What's Cooking, Alex?

Yvonne Coppard
Illustrated by Jan McCafferty

PUFFIN

PUFFIN BOOKS

Published by the Penguin Group
Penguin Books Ltd, 80 Strand, London WC2R 0RL, England
Penguin Group (USA), Inc., 375 Hudson Street, New York, New York 10014, USA
Penguin Books Australia Ltd, 250 Camberwell Road, Camberwell, Victoria 3124, Australia
Penguin Books Canada Ltd, 10 Alcorn Avenue, Toronto, Ontario, Canada M4V 3B2
Penguin Books India (P) Ltd, 11 Community Centre, Panchsheel Park,
New Delhi – 110 017, India
Penguin Group (NZ), cnr Airborne and Rosedale Roads, Albany, Auckland 1310, New Zealand
Penguin Books (South Africa) (Pty) Ltd, 24 Sturdee Avenue, Rosebank 2196, South Africa

Penguin Books Ltd, Registered Offices: 80 Strand, London WC2R 0RL, England

www.penguin.com

First published 2004
1

Set in 11.5/16pt Adobe Leawood

Made and printed in England by Clays Ltd, St Ives plc

British Library Cataloguing in Publication Data
A CIP catalogue record for this book is available from the British Library

ISBN 0-141-31802-3

PUFFIN BOOKS

WHAT'S COOKING, ALEX?

Yvonne Coppard was born in Ruislip, Middlesex, in 1955, the fourth of five children. Before becoming a full-time writer, she taught in London, Plymouth and Ely, then worked in child protection with the Cambridgeshire Local Education Authority. Married with two daughters, Yvonne lives just outside Cambridge. She loves reading, cinema, swimming, gossip (though not the vicious variety) and old buildings.

To the real Alexandra the Great

Chapter One

It all started three weeks ago. I was enjoying that last blissful five minutes in bed. You know, when you're only partly awake and almost ready to start the day, but you realize you've got time to snuggle down and have one more dream . . .

As I hand back one last autograph, I see the TV presenter making her way towards me along the red carpet, microphone in hand and camera in tow.

'Alexandra, you look absolutely stunning tonight. Can we ask who designed your dress?' she asks me.

'Actually, it's one of my own designs, Carla,' I reply modestly, doing a little twist so that the viewers can see every angle of my beautiful glittery gown. 'It's just a little

something I do in my spare time.'

'Tell our viewers, Alexandra, what's it like to be so talented and glamorous?' Carla gushes. 'And have you prepared your acceptance speech for tonight's award?'

'Oh, I don't expect to win anything,' I reply humbly, giving her a devastating smile.

I'm just about to move on to greet more of my adoring fans, when there's a sudden crash and my bedroom door flies open.

Wait a minute! My bedroom door? At a snazzy awards ceremony?

I opened my eyes to see my mum hopping in the doorway, pulling on a slipper with one hand and trying to brush her teeth with the other. My five-year-old brother, Evan, was in tow. He loves a bit of drama.

'Grrup! Gupp! Sssaytclerk!' Mum glared at me with a slightly mad expression. She's a nurse, and she's usually quite calm and sensible. My dad's the nutty one. Usually.

'Mum, you're not making any sense,' I said. 'What's up?'

She disappeared. There was a revolting sound of spitting and gargling from the bathroom, then she stormed back in. 'Get up! It's eight o'clock!'

I squinted at the clock by my bed. It said five to eight. 'No, it isn't. It's not even half past seven. Look.'

It's a well-known secret in our house that all the upstairs clocks are thirty minutes fast. My dad honestly believes that:

a) this will get us out of bed early, and
b) we don't know he's done it.

The truth is that we all know he's done it, even Evan! We all just work around it.

'Yes, it *is* eight o'clock! Someone's changed the clocks!' Mum shouted. 'Someone other than Dad, that is. Get up!'

I grabbed my watch. Mum was right. Eight o'clock. '*Aaaagh!*'

The next few minutes were complete chaos – 'Where're my school shoes . . . have you seen my reading bag . . . what's that dog doing with my *Nursing Magazine* . . .?' – the sort of stuff that goes on when your entire family gets up half an hour late.

'Who's left these shoes here? And move

these books!' yelled Mum, as she tripped over my school shoes then stubbed her toe on a pile of Dad's books that were propping the dining-room door open.

Just then, Dad appeared from his study, where he had probably worked all night (he keeps odd hours sometimes). He looked vaguely surprised to see us all rushing around, as he yawned his way towards the kitchen. 'Have you put the coffee on, love?' he asked Mum, rubbing his eyes.

Mum spluttered with rage before slamming the bathroom door.

'I'll do it, then, shall I?' he asked.

While Mum carried on getting ready for work, Dad sorted out some breakfast for Evan and me.

'We've been learning time at school,' Evan proudly announced, as jam from his doughnut dribbled down his chin. He looked at me and grinned. 'And d'you know what, Alex? The clocks upstairs were all wrong!' he said, his eyes all wide and innocent. 'So I made them the same as the clocks downstairs.'

'Evan, you –!' I was about to tell him exactly what I thought of him when Dad handed over another warmed-up, very-gooey doughnut. Little brothers last forever (unfortunately), but warm doughnuts need immediate attention. So I let Evan off. This time.

'What are you eating?' Mum came into the kitchen, dressed in her uniform with the buttons done up wrong and a hairbrush dangling from the side of her head. 'Martin, tell me those aren't doughnuts!'

'Those aren't doughnuts,' said Dad obligingly.

Evan and I saw Mum heading for our plates and quickly crammed everything we could into our mouths.

Mum glared at Dad, gave one of those huge sighs she saves for days when she feels really put upon, and got some yoghurt out of the fridge. 'What went wrong with the clocks, then?' she asked.

'It was Evan!' I pointed accusingly at him.

'I was only trying to help,'

he said, putting on his cute look for Mum. 'We're learning time at school, and I know all the half pasts and o'clocks now. And Miss Adams said we have to practise and practise. And the clocks upstairs were wrong!'

That cute look never fails.

'Well, never mind then,' cooed Mum. 'But next time you want to play with the clocks at home, ask me or Dad, OK?'

Evan nodded solemnly. Then he licked the dribbly jam off his chin, sticking his tongue out at me as he did so.

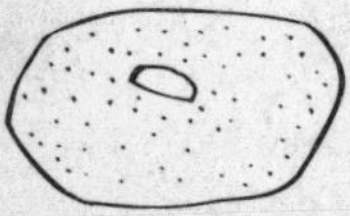

Back in history there was this horrible Russian ruler called Ivan the Terrible. Dad calls my brother Evan the Terrible when he's being naughty (which is most of the time). He sometimes calls me Alexandra the Great, after a bloke called Alexand*er* the Great – who was king of practically the whole world, I think. It must be because I have such great ideas – though Dad always seems to be grinning when he calls me A the G. Grown-ups are a mystery.

Now everyone was in a bad mood, except for Evan.

I guess five-year-olds don't worry too much about being late. I hadn't had time to lemon juice my freckles (someone told me it makes them fade, so I'm giving it a go). And I couldn't find my hairbrush, so I scraped my hair into a messy pony-tail with my fingers, hoping that Rosie (my best friend, who's a real whizz with hair) would do a French plait for me later.

Rosie would be wondering why I hadn't called for her by now. She'd have to walk to school without me if I didn't get there in the next five minutes.

No chance.

Our dog, Bear, sometimes decides he wants some company, so he lies down across the front door to stop us leaving. (Dad doesn't really count as company when he's locked away in his study.) Ever tried to heave a Newfoundland that weighs as much as your dad out of the way?

Mum did her big sigh again. 'Martin, get that piece of leftover ham from the fridge.'

I'm not sure if Bear knows the word 'ham' but he certainly looked interested, especially when he heard the sound of the fridge being opened. So he trundled off to investigate what

Dad was up to and we all slipped out of the door. We do that kind of thing a lot with Bear. Luckily, he's not clever enough to work it out and it's good that Dad works at home, so he can provide a decoy.

Dad's a writer, which people think is very glamorous, but he writes textbooks and magazine articles that make your eyes glaze over before you've got to the end of the title.

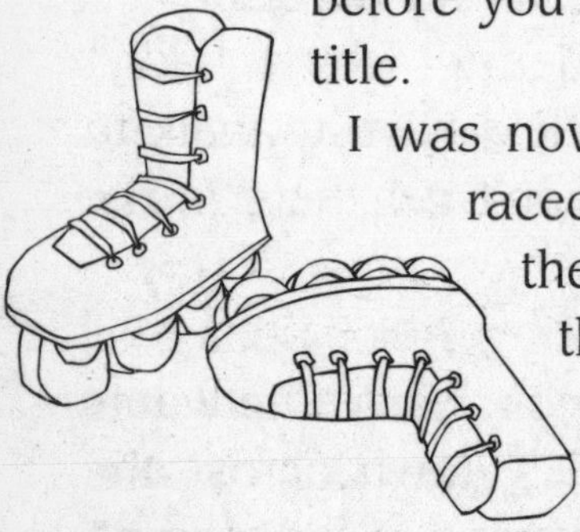

I was now ten minutes late, so I raced past Rosie's house at the end of my road and ran the rest of the way. I'd hoped to make up the time by rollerblading to school, but then Dad said that, until I can get to the end of the road without falling over, I'm not allowed.

I rushed through the corridors to my classroom and arrived all breathless and red-cheeked.

Miss Westrop made a big thing of looking at her watch. 'Good morning, Alexandra. I'm sure you have a good excuse?' she said.

I opened my mouth to tell her about Evan

and the clocks, but one of her stern looks told me it would be a waste of breath. 'I overslept. Sorry, Miss.'

'Well, go and sit down,' she said. 'You've got another late mark in the register – don't start a collection of them.'

I slunk over to my desk beside Rosie's. She shot a knowing look at my messy hair. 'I'll plait it for you at break,' she whispered.

Rosie's the best.

Pearl Barconi – spoiled princess and my sworn enemy – turned to smirk at me. 'You're really late,' she said. 'Miss is cross with you.'

Pearl is an expert at stating the obvious. Her real name is Pearl Barconi, but I call her Macaroni because her family got rich by selling pasta – and also because it annoys her. Just because her dad owns Barconi's, the swanky Italian restaurant in town, and her mum used to be a model, Pearl Barconi acts like she's royalty or something.

'It's part of the official protest,' I said. I took off my glasses and casually wiped them on my T-shirt, like I wasn't really taking much notice of her.

Pearl raised her eyebrows. 'What protest?' she asked.

Rosie joined in. She turned to Pearl and pretended to be dead surprised. 'You mean you don't know?' she asked, her dark curls bobbing around her face.

Macaroni loves gossip as much as Rosie and me. 'Know *what*?' she repeated.

Miss Westrop said, 'Sssh!' and wagged a finger at us, so we all looked down at our reading books.

We always start the day with silent reading. Miss Westrop reads too, to set a good example. But today she was reading *Hiya!* magazine, not her usual sort of book. I wondered if that meant I could read my comic, but decided not to risk it, especially as I was already in her bad books this morning.

I tapped my finger on my nose, looked at Pearl in the knowing sort of way that criminals and spies do on the TV, and put my glasses back on. I hoped it would drive her mad for the rest of the day, thinking there was something going on and she wasn't a part of it.

But Macaroni didn't bat an eyelid. She just said, 'Oh, secrets. I've got one of those. Haven't I?' She turned to Melissa, Tania and Kylie, who follow her about like adoring slaves. They smiled knowingly and nodded.

So it was Rosie and me who were left festering all morning.

As we were all lining up to go to lunch, Miss Ross, our headmistress, came into the classroom. Miss Ross used to be in the army and Dad is scared of her. Most of us kids think she's all right though. You just have to get used to her being a tidiness freak, that's all. She pointed at Josh's undone shoelace and frowned at Mina, who immediately took off her big bead necklace.

'Can we have a word, Miss Westrop?' asked Miss Ross. Then I noticed someone else standing in the doorway: Amber Barconi . . .

Hiya! magazine always describes Amber Barconi as a 'former celebrity model turned chef to the stars!' because her catering company makes food for all her famous friends' parties. I've always wondered how she manages to cook anything with those long, manicured nails. And she wears enough jewellery to sink a battleship. I bet bits of it drop off into the food sometimes. She's also Macaroni's mum.

Pearl gave her mum a little wave as we all trailed past, on our way down the corridor to the hall. Then she turned and smiled knowingly at her three groupies. They definitely had a secret. Grrrr. How frustrating.

Pearl opened up her lunchbox and took out a plate and a napkin.

'What have you got today, Pearl?' asked the fan club in unison.

Peering into her lunchbox with a superior little smile, Pearl replied, 'Let me see . . . Goats' cheese and red-onion relish on rye bread baked with poppy seeds, a little green salad . . . And to follow, fresh berries with black-currant and mint coulis, and a piece of lemon shortbread.'

'Oooohh . . . lovely!' the fan club simpered.

I looked at Rosie and we rolled our eyes at each other. Rosie's lunchbox is just like mine – sort of thrown together.

But we don't care. We rummaged around and swapped a sandwich each, like always. It's a good thing Mum had packed my lunch the night before, or I'd have had no lunch at all, what with the clocks fiasco!

'Peanut butter and jam,' said Rosie, sighing with pleasure at my sandwiches.

'Cheese and pickle – yum,' I said, biting into one of hers.

Macaroni looked over and pulled a face.

Swallowing my bite of sandwich, I cracked. Forcing myself not to call her Macaroni, I said, 'So, come on, Pearl – what's this great secret, then?'

Pearl shook her head to make her beautifully styled hair swing and catch the light. 'I can't tell,' she replied. 'Amber says it might not happen, and then everyone will be disappointed. So until it's all confirmed, I've promised not to say anything.'

Pearl calls her mum by her first name. How weird is *that*?

Rosie nodded at the fan club. 'But you've already told *them*,' she pointed out.

Macaroni smiled smugly. 'They're my special friends.'

Melissa, Tania and Kylie preened themselves like a bunch of prize-winning poodles.

'But the promise is broken now. So you may as well tell *us*,' I argued.

'Are you *so* desperate to know?' asked

Macaroni, pretending to be bored with the whole conversation, but loving it really.

'No!' Rosie and I both said together.

And we could hardly ask more questions when we were trying to pretend we were above it all. So that was that. We finished our sandwiches and hurried out into the playground.

'So . . . whatever the secret is, it involves Macaroni's mum . . .' Rosie mused, as she French plaited my hair.

I divided my last bit of chocolate in two, and handed her one chunk. We chomped together in miserable, frustrated silence.

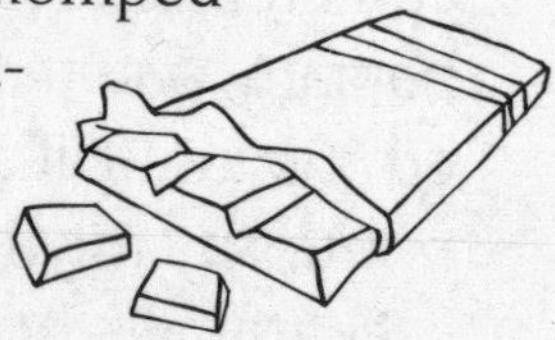

Five minutes later, Miss Ross and Miss Westrop strolled down the path towards the gate with Amber Barconi. They were all smiling and talking and doing a lot of arm waving. Something was definitely going on.

'Know what?' I said. 'I really need to go to the loo. Come on.'

The loos were across the playground, quite near to where the three of them stood chatting. So we 'accidentally' heard what they were saying.

'It will be such a wonderful opportunity for the class,' said Miss Westrop.

'Thank you so much for thinking of us, Amber,' said Miss Ross.

Amber treated them to a dazzling smile. 'I'm sure his people will be in touch soon,' she said.

Whose people? I could hardly *bear* it!

Then a taxi arrived to collect her, and Miss Ross and Miss Westrop waved her off like loyal subjects of the Queen. Looks like Macaroni isn't the only Barconi with a fan club!

Just then the bell rang and we all lined up to go back to the classroom.

As Miss Ross walked past, Pearl made sure everyone was listening, then puffed herself up importantly. 'Is it all settled now, Miss Ross?' she asked.

'See to your socks, Pearl,' Miss Ross instructed, ignoring the question.

Macaroni pulled up her socks and looked suitably put down.

Rosie and I did a high-five.

When we got back into the classroom, Miss Westrop told us to come and sit on the carpet.

'This is it . . .' I whispered to Rosie.

'I have some exciting news.' Miss Westrop

beamed. 'Our class is going to have an important visitor!'

We all groaned. That usually means a schools inspector or a governor, or someone equally boring.

'No, no!' she went on. 'I mean a *really* important visitor. A *celebrity*.'

We all stopped groaning.

'I'll give you three guesses who,' she said, watching our faces.

'Will Masters!' shouted out Macaroni immediately.

There was a big 'Oooohhhh!'

'Yes, Pearl, it's Will Masters,' Miss Westrop said tightly. She threw Pearl one of her dagger looks. 'Of course it's a bit of a cheat for you to guess, isn't it? What a pity you didn't give the others a chance.'

'Oh, sorry. Yes.' Pearl giggled. 'Because it's my mum who's organized it, you mean? I forgot.'

Nobody believed for a second that she'd forgotten, but we were all too stunned to speak. Will Masters, the TV chef! Even Mum has two of his cookery books, and cooking isn't usually her thing. Not only does he make cooking seem easy and fun in his TV programme, he is also gorgeous and funny and . . . gorgeous.

Then suddenly, we were all talking at once. 'Really, Miss?'. . . 'When, Miss?' . . . 'Why's he coming here, Miss?' . . . 'Are we going to be on the telly, Miss?'

When the fuss had died down a bit, Miss Westrop began to explain. 'Will is calling one of the programmes in his next series *Young Cooks of Tomorrow*,' she said. 'It's about inspiring young people to cook. Will was looking for a suitable class around your age to feature on his programme and Pearl's mother heard about this when she was a guest on his show –'

'A celebrity guest,' Pearl interrupted helpfully, 'because before she began to cook for exclusive parties, she used to be a top model, you know.'

'Really? I didn't know *that*!' Callum Kilroy is good at sarcasm. He looked around. 'Did anyone else hear about Pearl's mum being a top model?'

'Only about a hundred times,' said Charlotte, rolling her eyes.

Miss Westrop's mouth twitched, then she carried on. 'So, for the first part of his programme, Will is going to do a cookery demonstration right here in this school. And our class is going to be his audience. Then a couple of weeks later, you'll have the chance to show him what you've learned – you'll be filmed cooking a dish of your own for the second part of the programme. And Will is going to judge the results! Isn't that exciting, Class Six?'

Miss Westrop doesn't often get an answer to that question. Usually the exciting thing is a new set of textbooks or our turn to do assembly. Teachers find the weirdest things thrilling.

But I had to hand it to her this time. Will Masters at our school, looking for a Young Cook of Tomorrow. This was definitely exciting. This was my big chance to be discovered and get on TV. I could be on my way to making my favourite dream come true!

Chapter Two

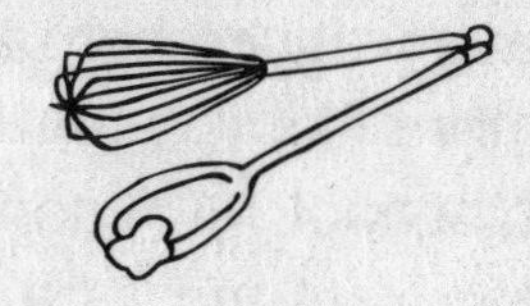

'I'm going to be famous,' I said.

We were all sitting round the kitchen table eating dinner. Mum insists that when she isn't working one of her weird shifts at the hospital, we have to 'sit down together to eat as a family'. She calls it 'quality time' or something. I call it missing all the decent telly.

'More sprouts, anyone?' said Mum.

'Good stuff,' said Dad.

'Sprouts are poo,' said Evan.

'No, Evan. Sprouts are vegetables,' said Dad. 'Pass that dish to me, would you?'

'Did anyone hear me?' I asked, a bit louder. 'I said I'm going to be famous.'

'You're always saying that,' said Evan. 'And you never *are* famous.'

I ignored him. 'Well, I'm going to be on the telly, anyway. That's the first step. Anyone heard of Will Masters?'

That certainly got Mum's attention. 'Will Masters?' she breathed. If she'd been a puppy, she would have wagged her tail.

That was more like it. I told them what had happened at school. 'So don't be surprised when Will discovers me as a Young Cook of Tomorrow pretty soon and asks me to be on his show every week,' I concluded.

Mum shrieked like a fan at a rock concert. 'You're joking! Will Masters, here in Derrington?'

The bit about me being a Young Cook of Tomorrow didn't seem to cut much ice, but the thought of Will Masters breathing the same air was enough to make Mum go all giggly.

Dad scowled. 'I don't know what the Will Masters fuss is about,' he sniffed. 'What with his fake tan and –'

'No way is that tan fake,' I interrupted.

Mum nodded. 'Alex is right. Look!' She dived for a magazine and opened it to show Will Masters on a jet ski.

SPORTY WILL PROVES HE'S MASTER OF THE MED said the headline.

'What's the Med?' I asked.

'The Mediterranean,' said Mum. 'He spends a lot of time there, doing water sports. That's where he gets his lovely tan,' she added dreamily.

Dad sniffed again. 'We could all look like that if we had his money,' he said.

'No, Dad,' chirped Evan, peering over Mum's arm to look at the picture. 'You could never look like that. You're much older than he is. And you're fatter.'

'Thanks, Evan. Good to know we men stick together,' said Dad. He glowered at Mum, who was trying not to laugh, and carried on eating.

Because Mum works such odd hours, she doesn't very often feel like cooking a meal from scratch. And Dad can't be trusted to. Once he's in his study it's as if the rest of the world has disappeared – including whatever's bubbling away on the hob or cooking in the oven. After the second time the neighbours had to call out the fire brigade, Mum decided it was safer to rely on convenience foods rather than Dad.

But the day after my announcement, the Will Masters cookbooks were out on the kitchen table and she was making a proper shopping list of ingredients. 'Do you think sun-blushed tomatoes are the same as sun-dried?' she asked Dad.

'No idea,' said Dad from behind his *History of Our Times* magazine. 'But do you really need to know in order to heat up the Mr Frosty Deluxe Pizza we usually have on a Thursday?'

'Hmm, well . . . I thought I'd have a go at this Will Masters pizza recipe instead,' Mum replied. 'The book says it only takes twenty minutes once you've got a pizza base . . .'

Dad looked a bit disgruntled, but said nothing. 'I've learned over the years never to question her when she's up to something,' he whispered to me. 'It always ends in an argument, and she always manages to win.'

'How do you know she *is* up to something?' I asked.

Dad held up a finger. 'First, she says "Hmmm, well . . .", then –' He held up a second finger – 'she squints with her right eye . . . like that.' He nudged me and nodded in Mum's direction.

Sure enough, Mum was leaning against the sideboard, squinting into the distance – evidently away with the fairies.

The next day, Mum forgot she didn't have time to cook. For dinner, we had Parma ham with grilled nectarines, followed by cheese and roast-pepper salad – all from one of the Will Masters cookbooks. It tasted OK, actually.

But Dad was determined not to be impressed. 'I thought this guy was supposed to be a *cook*.' He sniffed. 'Most of this stuff is practically raw.' He prodded the grilled nectarine then tore apart a bread roll.

'Will believes that you should choose the finest ingredients and muck about with them as little as possible. The natural taste and texture should just *burst* through,' said Mum enthusiastically.

'He's not daft, is he?' said Dad. 'I wish I could

find fame and fortune by slinging a few uncooked ingredients on a plate and convincing people they want to eat it.'

'Martin, you're not jealous of Will, are you?' said Mum, raising her eyebrows.

'*What?*' Dad spluttered. 'As Alex would say, Puh-*lease* . . .'

But I could see from the way Mum was smiling that she didn't believe him. Then she turned to me. 'You know, Alex,' she said casually, 'I've been thinking about the cookery demonstration. Do you know what arrangements have been made for First Aid? Lots of inexperienced children, ovens, naked flames, sharp knives . . . who knows what could happen!'

'Oh, Miss Westrop talks about safety all the time,' I replied. 'I'm sure it will be taken care of.'

Mum shook her head doubtfully. 'By some amateur with a bit of sticky plaster and a tube of antiseptic cream probably,' she said dismissively. 'I bet they would prefer to have someone more skilled, if they could. A qualified and experienced nurse, for example.'

The awful truth hit me like a thunderbolt and I stopped chewing my nectarine. I went hot, then cold, then hot again. *Please, no*, I thought. *Don't do this to me.*

'What are you saying, Mum?' I asked.

She looked at me with a big smile. I knew exactly what was coming next.

'Tomorrow,' she said, 'I'm going to the school to offer my services.'

Chapter Three

I'm not saying I'd rather die than have my mum in school, throwing herself at Will Masters, but I'd rather have a boil on the end of my nose and a cross-eyed squint. Two cross-eyed squints. And give my new purple trainers to Pearl. Or . . . well, you get the picture.

'No way,' I said.

'Why not?' said Mum sniffily. 'Evan, *do* try to chew your food properly.'

'That means more than once, Evan,' added Dad, as Evan sucked up some spinach leaves and swallowed.

Watching Evan eat is something you could sell tickets for. Fastest gobbler, grossest table dribbler – he'd win any contest you care to put him in. I hoped Mum might get sidetracked into one of her lectures on The Importance of Good Table Manners, but no.

'Why not?' she repeated.

'It's just not . . . Mums don't . . . the other kids would . . .'

She was looking me square in the eye and I couldn't go through with it.

'She thinks you'll go all gooey when you see Will Masters. And that it'll be really embarrassing!'

I hadn't opened my mouth, but the exact words in my head were suddenly out there. Evan the Terrible, for once, had come to my rescue. He was still chomping away like a hyperactive tortoise, with little bits of dinner stuck to his chin.

'Evan's right, Julie,' Dad agreed. 'Alex is at a particularly sensitive age for feeling embarrassed by parents . . .'

I nodded enthusiastically.

'. . . as well as freckles, glasses, clumsiness . . .'

'All right, all right, Dad,' I interrupted. 'No need to go on.'

But he went on anyway. 'In other words, Alex is at the point where she needs to start carving her own identity. To be seen as an individual rather than someone else's child . . .'

Mum's mouth was wide open. 'Where did you get all *that* from?' she asked.

'*Parent Monthly*.' Dad smiled proudly. 'I'm writing a column for them while their regular writer is away, so I thought I'd better read a few issues. It's coming in quite handy!'

Mum turned to me. 'So what you're saying is, you're ashamed of me,' she said.

'No!' I denied. 'Well, not exactly.'

'Yep!' said Evan.

'Of course she is,' grinned Dad.

'Well . . .' Mum seemed half hurt, half indignant and half amused. (Yes, I know that equals $1\frac{1}{2}$.)

Escape was in sight, so I relaxed a bit. 'Tell you what, Mum. I'll get you Will Masters' autograph,' I offered generously.

Mum looked a bit more forgiving. 'And a photo,' she bargained.

'A what? How am I supposed to –?' I saw her expression and gave in. 'Yeah, right, OK,' I agreed. I'd get the photo somehow.

'You needn't think it's going on view, this photo,' said Dad grumpily. 'As if there aren't enough pictures of him splattered across the papers every day . . .'

'Get me a signed photo, and it's a deal,' said Mum, ignoring him.

And that was that. Phew!

The night before Will Masters was coming into school, I took over the bathroom. I squeezed three whole lemons and painted the juice on my freckles. You have to leave it on overnight for best effect. Some of it ran into my ears and up my nose, which was gross, but if you want fame, you have to pay the price.

My skin was really tight and itchy in the morning. But when I looked in the mirror, I was sure the freckles were paler.

Wearing my lucky striped T-shirt, I went to Rosie's a bit early so that she could do my hair in a lovely French plait.

'You look great,' said Rosie.

'So do you,' I said, trying not to sound jealous. You don't have to stretch the truth when you say something like that to Rosie. Her dark curly hair never looks straggly like mine always does. And she's got big brown eyes and lovely toffee-coloured smooth skin.

Rosie's fingers moved like lightning as I told her about Dad being jealous of Will, and how he came out with all that magazine stuff about children needing their parents to stay out of their way. 'He only agreed with the magazine because *he* didn't want Mum up at the school batting her eyelashes at Will, either!' I said. 'Parents!'

Rosie rolled her eyes in sympathy.

When we got to school, most of our class was already in the playground. Everyone was really excited and seemed to have made an effort to look good as they were going to be on telly.

But if Dad's article was right, then Macaroni Barconi

sure has problems! She and her mum turned up wearing identical pink designer jeans and T-shirts. Pearl was even wearing the same lipstick!

Amber Barconi seemed to think *she* was the reason everyone had made an effort to look their best. She walked through the playground smiling and greeting people like she was a film star at the opening of her latest movie.

'Your hair could be *soooo* pretty, with a little bit of effort, darling,' I heard her coo to Kerry Marsden, the toughest girl in our class. 'Why don't you ask Mummy to buy you some *nice pink* slides to bring out those lovely red highlights?' she suggested.

Kerry, who once said she would rather wear nothing than wear pink, looked like she was about to be sick on Amber's *nice pink* jeans.

The rest of us were saved from Amber's beauty tips by the appearance of Miss Ross on the other side of the playground.

'Excuse me, girls,' Amber trilled. 'I must just go and have a word about how we're managing the morning. I'll catch you later, Pearl, darling.'

Amber and Pearl smiled at each other and sort of kissed the

air near each other's cheeks. Two big mouths, two sets of perfect white teeth (no tooth would dare stand out of line in a Barconi mouth) and pouty brown lipstick. Then Amber was gone.

Rosie groaned. 'Did you hear what she said? Managing the morning? That means she's staying.'

'Yuk,' I said.

'Don't be so rude,' said Melissa. She and the other two members of the Macaroni Fan Club glared at us, bristling like a gaggle of hairy geese.

'I think Amber's just amazing, Pearl,' simpered Tanya.

Kylie nodded. 'So do I,' she said.

Pearl bestowed a smile upon them, then linked arms with Melissa and they stalked off.

When the bell went, we all lined up as usual.

Miss Ross was on duty. Rosie suggested she'd arranged it deliberately so that she could escape from Amber for a few minutes.

'Pearl, what is that on your mouth?' Miss Ross asked, frowning.

'Burnt Kiss,' said Pearl proudly. 'It's Amber's, really, but she said as it's a special day I could –'

'Not in *my* school you can't,' Miss Ross said.

'Go and wash it off. At once.'

Macaroni went positively tomato-coloured and stomped off to the lavatories.

As the rest of us walked in a line to our classroom, I could hear the fan club twittering, '*Ooh, it's not fair! Poor Pearl. Never mind, she looks lovely without lipstick . . .*'

Good start to the day.

Miss Westrop wasn't in the classroom yet, so we all carried on chatting, wondering what Will would be like, and when he'd turn up.

'OK, Class Six, settle down!'

'Wow!' said Rosie, as Miss Westrop walked into the classroom.

'*Phwoah!*' said one of the boys.

'That's enough, Class Six! It's only a haircut,' Miss Westrop said, but I could tell that she was secretly pleased. Her hair was cut into a new style and it looked all glossy and smooth. She had a new dress too, a soft red one that wasn't like anything she usually wears.

'But you look *lovely*, Miss,' said Rosie.

'Thank you, Rosie,' Miss Westrop replied. 'Now, what an exciting day ahead!' she went on. 'We need a couple of representatives from Class Six to greet Will Masters when he arrives. Any volunteers?'

My hand shot up straight away. So did Pearl's.

'Right. First two hands up were Alexandra and Pearl. Come and see me after the register.'

Great – I got stuck with Macaroni. Just my luck.

Will was due to arrive after assembly. So when everyone else went back to the classroom, Pearl and I made our way to the back gates with Miss Ross. A small crowd had gathered on the other side – word that Will Masters was expected must have got around.

Mr Manick, the school caretaker, was standing guard, holding a broom. 'Stay back,' he ordered the crowd. 'Stay back, I tell you!'

'I think we're safe without the broom today, Mr Manick,' said Miss Ross crisply. 'I don't think they're going to stampede.'

Mr Manick looked a bit disappointed. I think Mr Manick is a bit mad, to tell the truth. But he does take very good care of the school. He also looks old enough to be most people's great-great-great grandad. So he makes a great Santa for the little ones on the last day of term before Christmas.

Just then, Pearl pointed into the crowd. 'Oh, look! That's your *mother*, isn't it, Alex?' she asked, her eyebrows raised.

I laughed dismissively. 'No, *my* mum wouldn't dream of . . .' My eyes followed Pearl's pointing finger and my stomach dropped into my trainers. It *was* Mum. 'Oh, I see who you mean,' I added hurriedly. 'It does *look* a bit like my mum. But it's not though. She's at work today.'

I could tell Pearl didn't believe me. She opened her mouth to say more – but just then a TV trailer rolled up outside the school gates.

The crowd of fans erupted into cheers as Will leaned out of the passenger window and waved.

Mr Manick sprang into action and opened the gates. Unable to resist using his broom, he waved it menacingly at the crowd, herding them out of the way as if they were sheep. 'Right. Come on now, step back. Step back, I say! Let 'em through!'

The trailer moved into the playground and Mr Manick closed the gates behind it with a loud clang.

As Will and his assistant jumped down from the cabin of the trailer, Miss Ross hurried forward to greet them. Cameras in the crowd began clicking and flashing like mad.

'Alex! Alex, over here!' An urgent stage whisper came from the woman I was trying to pretend wasn't my mum.

I ignored her.

'Alex, it's me! Over here!' Mum beckoned.

Macaroni smirked. But just then, Amber, who looked like she'd applied another three coats of Burnt Kiss to her mouth, came charging towards us like a rhino.

'Will, darling!' she gushed. 'How lovely to see you again.' She grabbed Will by the shoulders and gave him a smacking great kiss on each cheek.

Will looked a bit surprised. 'Oh, hi, Amber. How's it going?' he said casually.

Then Pearl, who had now forgotten all about my embarrassing mother, stepped forward. 'Will, how lovely to meet you.' She stretched out her hand. 'I do hope you had a pleasant journey?' She sounded like the queen.

'My daughter, Pearl,' said Amber proudly. 'She and . . . er, her little friend here will help you find anything you need.'

Will smiled, then took Macaroni's hand and shook it solemnly. You could see he was trying not to laugh. The woman with him was having trouble too.

Will turned to me and stretched out his hand. 'And you are . . .?'

I just blushed. 'Oh, er, Alex. Hi, Will.' Inside, I kicked myself. I looked completely stupid. Then I saw my mother, still trying to dodge past Mr Manick's broom, and I knew for sure where I inherited *that* from.

'Let's go in, shall we?' said Miss Ross. 'Alex, you lead the way.'

Breathing a sigh of relief, I hurried towards the school hall before my mother could identify herself as being anything to do with me.

I caught sight of myself in a mirror. My French plait was already coming loose on one side, my glasses were crooked and a black smudge had appeared on my T-shirt. How it got there, I have no idea. Macaroni, of course, was immaculate.

The rest of the class were waiting for us in the hall with Miss Westrop.

'And this is Class Six's teacher, Miss Westrop,' Miss Ross told Will.

'Miss Westrop, a pleasure to meet you. Do call me Will – everyone does,' said Will. 'And may I say, what a lovely red dress!'

Miss Westrop's face did a good job of matching it. 'Well, thank you, Will – and d-do call m-me Angelina,' she stuttered.

We were all allowed to sit and watch as Will's crew set up the equipment in the hall, ready for cooking and filming. There were three cameras – huge things on trolleys, with lots of cables and lights. The camera operators hopped about from place to place, shifting lights, moving bits of furniture and signalling to each other with strange hand movements. Rosie and I tried to suss out the best spot to get ourselves on television.

Finally, everything was ready and Will asked

us to gather round his huge table, which was crammed with cooking equipment. 'OK,' he said. 'Before the cameras start to roll, just a quick tip: the cameras will pan – that means come round – the audience now and then. Ignore them. Just act normally.'

'Anyone waving at the camera or making silly faces will have to sit in the corner and read instead,' added Miss Westrop fiercely.

'Thank you, Angelina.' Will grinned. 'Right, let's roll the cameras and have some fun!'

From out of nowhere came a soundtrack of music, then voices shouting out together, '*What's cooking, Will?*'

'Hello!' said Will to the camera. 'Welcome to *What's Cooking, Will?* This week's programme is all about getting kids to take an interest in cooking. After all, it's kids like Class Six here, at Derrington Primary School, who will become our cooks of tomorrow!'

The cameras started to 'pan' round us and

we all tried to look cool. I hope I did better than most of the others, who looked pretty goofy.

'So today I'm going to try and inspire them to have a go!' Will went on. 'I'll be preparing a few simple but totally scrummy dishes. And, later in the programme, we'll see how Class Six fare when they're let loose in a kitchen themselves! So watch carefully, kids. Here goes . . .'

'Alex, what's the matter?' Rosie hissed.

'Nothing. What do you mean?' I turned away from the camera, which had just caught my best dramatic look.

'You look funny . . . do you need to go to the loo or something?'

So much for the dramatic look.

Princess Pearl was practically dangling from Camera 2, batting her eyelashes at the poor cameraman who was trying very hard to ignore her.

'Macaroni, have you got something in your eye?' I whispered. But it came out a bit louder than I'd intended. A few people laughed and Pearl gave me a dirty look.

'Alexandra Bond!' shouted Miss Westrop. 'No talking!'

'Don't worry,' said Will. 'We can edit that bit out.' But as he turned back to his demonstration he winked at me! He is *sooooo* gorgeous.

Will made everything look really easy. A handful of stuff tossed in the pan here, and twirl of a spoon there, and soon the hall was filled with smells that made everyone's mouth water. He threw ingredients into the air and they landed in whichever pan he wanted. He chopped things so fast we could barely see the knife – he even juggled with the eggs. And all the time he carried on talking – little jokes, tips and comments about how you could vary the ingredients and flavours.

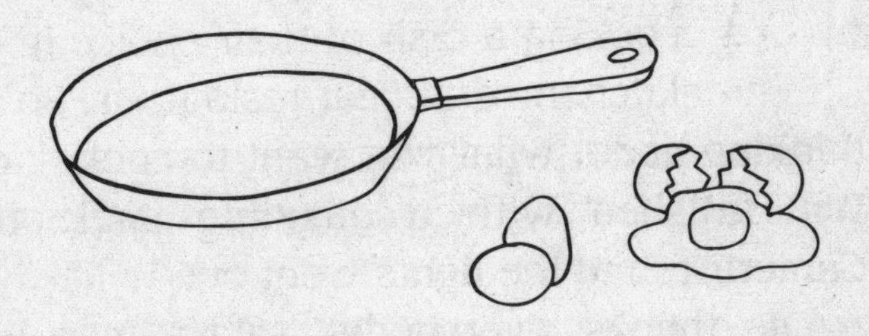

Finally it was over, and slices of delicious spicy omelette and tiny nests of meringue filled with strawberry stuff were being handed around so everyone could have a taste. It was delicious!

That is going to be me one day, I

thought dreamily. I could just picture it . . .

'Oh, Alex! This food is just so amazing. And you make it look so easy! They don't call you Alexandra the Great for nothing . . .'

'Oi, Alex!'

A sharp pain in the ribs, caused by Rosie's elbow, brought me back to reality.

Rosie grinned. 'Earth calling Alex – Will's about to tell us something important, so listen up.'

'Join us after the break when we'll see how Class Six put what they've learned into action! They'll be cooking a dish of their choice in the kitchen of a local restaurant. So get thinking about what you want to cook, kids!' Will finished with a dazzling smile into Camera 1, and the lights went out.

'OK, thanks, everybody!' said a man with a clipboard who we'd been told was the producer.

'Well, that was very inspiring!' said Miss Westrop. 'I hope you're all now bursting with ideas about what to cook for Will when he films you at Barconi's restaurant.'

Rosie and I looked at each other. It had to be Barconi's, didn't it?

Pearl and Amber beamed with pride.

'What's more,' Miss Westrop went on, 'Will has told me that there will be a prize for the best dish. So I suggest you get practising!'

Will smiled. 'I just know you're going to come up with something brilliant,' he said, looking straight at me. (Rosie and Jane and Jasminder all said afterwards that he was looking straight at *them*, but what do they know?)

I just knew my destiny was to be discovered by Will Masters, and be a famous chef, up there on stage with him. It would go something like this . . .

'So, Alex, what are we cooking today?'

'Today, Will, I thought we'd have a go at . . .'

OK, so my imagination couldn't come up with an actual dish, but that was just a matter of practice, wasn't it? 'One step at a time, Alex,' I told myself.

Step number one was clear. I had to win that competition.

'Alex, it was fate that made us choose Derrington Primary for that programme. There you were, the greatest cook ever to

walk the planet, just waiting to be discovered.'

'That's very kind of you, Will,' I say. 'But I learned everything I know from you. If you hadn't made me a regular guest on your show . . .'

They had been happy days, I reflect. From the start, Will had noticed something special in me. He had taken an interest in my talent, and finally asked me to be co-host of What's Cooking, Will? *with him. Who could have known, in those early days, that I would go on to have my own TV show and be even more famous than Will himself?*

'And you didn't forget your friends, Alex,' says Will. 'It was you inviting me to guest on your show that saved my career when I got too old to be gorgeous.'

'You'll always be gorgeous to me, Will.' I smile as I leave for my photo shoot with Hiya! *magazine . . .*

'Alexandra, are you listening?' Miss Westrop's voice brought me back to earth with a jump. 'Please take Will and the crew to the staffroom. Miss Johnson should be waiting there with coffee for them.'

Fame would have to wait a while.

Chapter Four

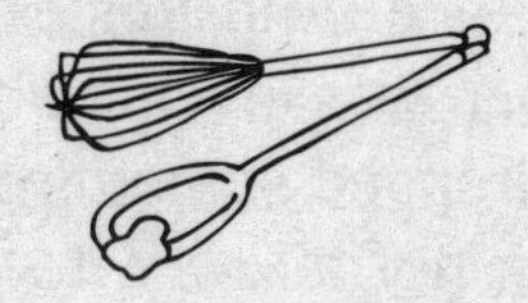

Rosie and I raced back from school to my house. We sometimes experimented in the kitchen, trying out weird flavour combinations in sandwich fillings and pizza toppings – stuff like that. But now we had some really serious work to do.

My house is best for experimenting because, as long as Mum's at work and Dad's safely tucked away in his study, we can pretty much do as we like in our kitchen. And we have Bear on hand to taste test and to hoover up any disgusting bits.

Rosie and I have had our share of disasters in the past – our worst being a mayonnaise and mint-sauce cake. But we've

also had some triumphs. My Alaska Surprise for instance: French toast, sandwiched together with jam and ice cream. Yum. Even Evan the Terrible eats it without pulling a face. And Rosie's Fizzy Apricot Pudding – which was invented by mistake. She accidentally dropped something into the apricot sauce (I'm not allowed to say what) that made it fizz in our mouths. And we liked it so much it's become her secret ingredient!

Rosie must have read my mind. 'You know, Alex, I think I might stick to my Fizzy Apricot Pudding for the competition,' she said.

I nodded. 'Mmm, good idea,' I said. 'But my best recipe is Alaska Surprise and it's too easy. It won't impress Will Masters. I'll have to create something new.' After all, you don't get to be a top TV chef with French toast. No, I needed something new, grown-up. With a foreign name. And exotic ingredients.

When Rosie went home, I was still trying to think of something. I got down the family collection of cookbooks for inspiration.

'Collection' sounds good, doesn't it? But there's not much. Cooking isn't Mum or Dad's thing. The two Will Masters cookbooks that

Mum had been given as birthday and Christmas presents were great, but I couldn't really use a Will Masters recipe for a contest he was judging! That left *Festive Fare Through the Ages* and *Susie Swanky's Christmas Party.* Oh, and Dad's filthy old student cookbook from centuries ago – *Nosh for Next to Nothing.*

At least *Festive Fare Through the Ages* looked interesting. Dad says they ate a lot of very sweet and very spicy food in olden times to disguise the fact that the meat was rotting, since they didn't have fridges. And Christmas mince pies actually had meat in them. Yuk! And I didn't fancy jellied pork brawn ('Take ½ a pig's brain . . .'). But I liked the look of Marbled Cream – fresh cream and berries and sugar mixed with rosewater. I thought I could do something with that. The picture looked lovely.

Mum had already said she would get me some ingredients on her way home, so I told her what I needed.

She raised her eyebrows at the rosewater. 'I'll give it a try,' she said doubtfully. 'But don't raise your hopes on my finding that one at the local supermarket.'

'And fresh raspberries would be nice,' I suggested.

'Fresh raspberries would be lovely,' agreed Mum. 'Unfortunately they would also cost a fortune – and that's if I can even find them in the shops at this time of year. There's some frozen blackberries in the freezer that we picked in the park.'

'Oh, Mum!' I protested. 'You always say we should do the very best we can, whatever the job. Fresh raspberries will make all the difference.'

'Well,' said Mum, 'if you feel that strongly about it –'

'I do, I really do!' I said firmly.

'– then you can pay for them with your own pocket money,' said Mum.

'On the other hand,' I said quickly, 'since raspberries would be so difficult for you to get hold of, I might as well use the blackberries.'

The following afternoon, after school, I lined up all my ingredients on the work surface. Mum hadn't been able to get me rosewater – so I'd decided to make my own. I mean, there's roses and there's water. So you just mix the two together. That had to be right. Right?

I picked the heads off a few roses from the garden and crumbled the petals into a bowl then poured on some water. It didn't look very appetizing. And it smelled more like perfume than food. But maybe that's what rosewater was *supposed* to be like.

There weren't quite enough blackberries left in the freezer, so I had the idea of putting in some chocolate and chopped nuts as well. They're great with almost anything, in my opinion. (Anything desserty, I mean. I wouldn't try them with battered fish or lamb stew.)

There weren't any in the kitchen cupboards, but I knew that Dad always keeps a container of mixed nuts and a bar of chocolate in his study for when he works through the night. I went to see if I could scrounge some.

'Here you go,' he said, handing it over. 'Delighted to do my bit in the cause of fame and fortune. What are you making?'

I explained about the recipe and my changes to it.

'So, an original Alexandra the Great creation, eh?' said Dad. 'What will you call it?'

'It's called Marbled Cream in the book,' I said. 'But I'm going to give it a new and exciting twist. And then I'll give it an exotic foreign name.'

Dad scratched his ear thoughtfully. 'Something French, perhaps,' he said.

'Any suggestions?' I asked.

'Mmm, let me see,' he said. 'How about . . . *Crème Mystique*? It means mysterious cream, which sounds exactly like what you're making.'

I liked it. 'Thanks, Dad.'

'Any time,' he said, and turned back to his computer.

They didn't have food processors in olden times. They had to chop and stir everything by hand – which was just as well, since Mum said I could only use the food processor if she was there to supervise.

It's a real downer trying to be creative with your mum watching everything you do. So I'd said, 'No, it's all right. I want to do it exactly the way they did in olden times.'

I lined everything up and made a start. Ages later, my cream was still runny and my blackberries were still bitty rather than smooth, and so were my chocolate and nuts. My hands felt like they were going to drop off!

I looked at the food processor. If I bunged everything in that and whizzed it round, it would take five seconds, ten tops . . .

What harm could it do? If I washed everything up carefully, Mum would never know.

I chopped another nut and cut my finger. Well, almost. It's impossible to *actually* cut your finger on the blunt knives Mum lets me use. But, anyway, I concluded that sort of proved that the food processor would be safer, so I decided to go for it.

I loaded the blackberries in with the cream and sugar, lumps of chocolate and nuts – and three handfuls of smelly, soggy rose petals. Then I put on the lid and, peering down into what was about to become my new masterpiece, I pressed 'On'.

How was I supposed to know that you *have* to cover the hole in the lid with that odd plastic bit?

In a second, the nearby wall and tiles and floor – not to mention me – were splattered with purply pink cream, bits of frozen blackberry, chocolate and nuts.

Evan had peeled himself away from the telly to see what the noise was. 'Wow! Looks like pink sick!' he said, delighted. His eyes were round as saucers as he took it all in. 'I'm going to get Dad to come and see . . .'

'Don't you dare, Evan. Get out of the kitchen,' I said.

'I want to watch,' he insisted. He tried to reach the 'On' switch again, and I shoved him out of the door.

Bear was pretty excited too. Tail wagging, he took a big lick of the new snack on the floor. His tail went still. Then he shook his huge head and sneezed. And sneezed again. The rose petals, maybe? In all the years that I'd known Bear, I'd never once found a food he didn't like – until now. He began to slide

himself along the kitchen floor, wiping his mouth on the rug. His thick coat mopped up the rest of the purply cream on the floor along the way.

Crème Mystique travels further than you would think when it is sneezed out by a Bear-sized dog.

'Bear!' I screamed. I opened the back door. 'Out!'

He looked at me, then sat down and shook his head again, as if to say, '*I'm* not going out into the cold – it's all *your* fault.'

'What's up now?' said Evan, poking his head round the door again. 'Oh, even more wow! You're gonna be in big trouble if Mum sees . . .'

'Shut up, Evan,' I said. 'Just help me get Bear out and then we can clear this mess up.'

Evan thought for a second. Then he said, 'Can't. I'm too little to do clearing up. And anyway I'm not Evan. I'm Banana Man . . .' And he went back to the telly.

I called Rosie in a panic. 'Mum will be home from work in two hours and Dad could come out of his study any minute and Evan says he can't help because he's Banana Man . . .' I was trying not to cry.

'I'll come round,' said Rosie.

*

'Ooh, Alex,' Rosie said, looking round at the kitchen, three minutes later. She ran a finger through one of the purply pink smears of Crème Mystique on the wall. It was beginning to dry, which made it even stickier. 'Ooh, Alex.'

For a moment I thought I had finally done something Rosie couldn't handle. But then she took a deep breath and opened the back door. 'Bear, out!' she said.

Bear trundled out into the garden and stood miserably with his nose pressed against the window. Bear knows better than to mess with Rosie – who can be really fierce when she wants to be.

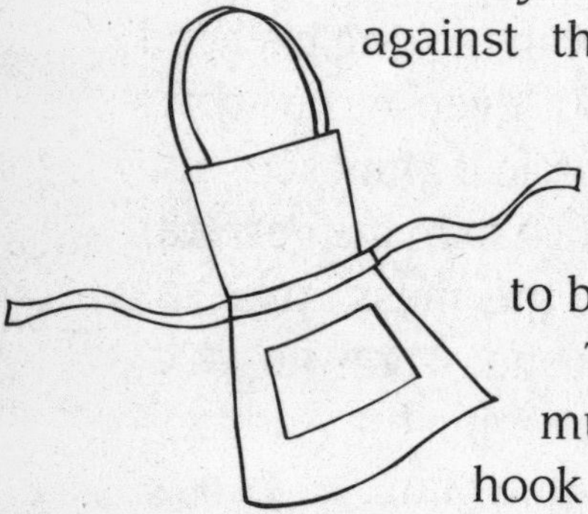

Then Rosie grabbed my mum's aprons from the hook on the door and threw one at me. 'Start with the wall,' she said. 'Let's get it off before it sets. Then the tiles. I'll sponge the rug.'

We were hard at it when Dad put his head round the door. 'Never knew cooking could be so noisy,' he said. 'Everything OK?'

'Fine, Dad, just made a bit of a mess,' I said.

'Right-o,' he said, and went back to his study.

Bear kept whining to remind us he was there. I fed him a ginger nut through the window, which cheered him up. For about three seconds.

We got the kitchen cleaned up with twenty minutes to spare before Mum was due back from work.

'Brilliant, Rosie!' I said. 'We did it!' Then a mournful '*Rouf!*' reminded me that we hadn't finished yet.

We looked through the kitchen window at Bear. His muzzle was still covered in pink drool and a rose petal was half stuck on his nose. His coat was sticky with dried-on *Crème Mystique*. He sneezed pitifully, spraying the kitchen window.

'Oh, lovely,' said Rosie.

My heart sank. In summer Bear likes being bathed. But being showered with a cold garden hose on a blustery autumn day was not something he was going to take lying down. Or sitting up. Or in any position that would make it easy to wash him.

He charged about, spraying water and dog shampoo everywhere. (I hope plants don't mind that stuff, because a fair bit of it landed on them.) And Rosie and I ended up as soapy as him. Soapier, probably.

'What on earth have you two been up to?' Mum arrived home as we were chasing Bear around the garden.

'Playing in the park,' I said. I have what Rosie calls a real talent for quick thinking. And stretching the truth. 'We were playing a sort of treasure-hunt game and Bear went dashing off into a muddy patch under the blackberry bushes. So we had to rescue him and give him a shower to get all the mud and blackberries off.'

'Oh Bear, honestly!' said Mum. 'Thanks for bathing him. And you've tidied up the kitchen too. That's brilliant. You're both stars.'

I smiled and shrugged. 'No problem, Mum.' Then I noticed Rosie was staring up at the kitchen ceiling just above Mum's head. I looked too. A glob of *Crème Mystique* was hanging there. We both looked at each other in panic. It could drop any minute . . .

'Why don't you go and sit down, Mum?' I said. 'Rosie and I will make you a cup of tea.'

Mum looked even more surprised. 'Hmm. Maybe I should take your temperature,' she joked. But she left the kitchen and we sighed with relief.

'Maybe you should cook something not so messy,' Rosie advised later, as we sat in my room eating Dad's leftover chocolate. 'And everyone seems to be doing desserts. What about something savoury?' she suggested. 'What's your favourite *savoury* food?'

'Cheese scones,' I said, without even having to think.

Cheese scones have been top of my list ever since I first had one on holiday in Devon with Mum and Dad when I was three. (Evan hadn't been born yet. Life was much more peaceful then.) Mum and Dad chose scones with strawberry jam and clotted cream – a proper Devon cream tea – but I had just found out that I liked cheese. Cheese scones are still my favourite – though I'd never tried to make them.

'Rosie,' I said, 'You are a genius. Cheese scones. But with a few extra unusual ingredients, of course. That's what I'll do.'

So Rosie went home, and I began to make a

list of what I could put into my scones to make them different enough to catch Will's eye.

Scones with a difference:
~~Cheese and onion~~ Too ordinary
~~Cheese and cherries~~ Too weird
Cheesy and curry powder? Mmm . . . maybe
Cheese and herb? Ask Mum/Dad about exotic ones
~~Cheese with a herby ice-cream filling~~ Yuk! Too far
Crunchy earwig scones (just for Evan)

Chapter Five

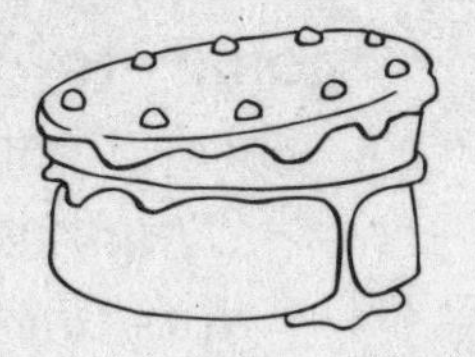

Rosie brought me some of her practice Fizzy Apricot Pudding in her packed lunch the next day. But the sauce had lost its fizz. So it was just Apricot Pudding really. But it tasted lovely anyway.

'You have to eat it straight away to taste the fizz, that's the problem,' said Rosie thoughtfully. 'I'll have to get the timing right for the competition. But, then, I don't really care about winning, since I don't want to be a chef when I grow up,' she went on. 'I want to be hairdresser.'

'Well *I'm* going to be a chef – but I don't even have a dish yet!' I pointed out.

Rosie licked the last few crumbs of Unfizzy Apricot Pudding from her fingers. 'I bet all the chefs we see on telly had to do much more than get covered in rose and chocolate mush and showered with dog shampoo before they reached perfection,' she said.

That cheered me up. Rosie was right. And when I'm rich and famous, I'm going to tell everyone about Rosie's salon.

Thank you so much for this Chef of the Century Award. I would like to thank my best friend, Rosie – who, in my darkest hour, reminded me that the dawn always comes . . . And yes, she did this amazing hairstyle for me, thanks for asking . . .

I was quite impressed with that. I've written it down so I won't forget it. Maybe I should think about becoming a famous writer instead . . .

Mum had given me money for a whole new batch of ingredients – as a thank you for cleaning Bear. So Rosie and I stopped at the corner shop on the way home.

'I need something exotic,' I told Mrs Runce.

She has run the corner shop ever since I can remember.

'Exotic? Hmm, I'll do my best,' she said. 'What's it for, pet?'

I explained about the competition and my ideas for exotic scones, and she got together a little batch of things. 'You could have a bash with these,' she said. 'There's bound to be something there you'll like, I reckon.'

Rosie and I left the shop with:

caraway seeds
fennel seeds
ground cardamoms
multi-coloured peppercorns
a bunch of fresh coriander

The combined smells were weird, but we agreed it all smelled very exotic.

I got home just about the same time as Mum. She was unpacking some bulging carrier bags, helped by Evan, who was hoping to find some biscuits.

'It's not supermarket day, is it?' I said, surprised.

'No,' Mum replied. 'But as I've got a bit of

time to spare, I thought I'd do some more proper cooking.'

'Sausage and chips?' said Evan hopefully.

Mum frowned. 'No, Evan. Another Will Masters recipe, actually. Something new and exciting.'

'Oh.' Evan trailed off mournfully, clutching his comic.

The 'something new and exciting' turned out to be Oriental Chicken Parcels. I have to admit that it looked and tasted good. But there wasn't a lot of it.

'That was quite tasty,' said Dad grudgingly. 'Good to know that Masters bloke has a few proper recipes up his sleeve. What's for dinner?'

Mum's face darkened. 'That *was* dinner.'

'No, I mean main course,' Dad explained. 'That must have been a starter, right?'

'Wrong,' said Mum. She gathered up our plates with a clatter. 'I made exactly what the recipe said, and it says it feeds four.'

'Ah . . .' said Dad. 'Um . . . Anyone fancy a hunk of cheese?'

Evan was looking through the cookbook and found the recipe. 'Here it is, look. It's just like the picture, Mummy.' He was full of admiration.

I had a look. Yes, Mum had done Will Masters proud. But then I turned back a page. Dad, looking over my shoulder, also saw the title of the chapter the recipe had come from. 'Super Starters'. Dad and I looked at each other. But we said nothing.

After eating my cheese, I found a scone recipe in Will's first cookbook, *Will Masters: The Basics*. Then I laid out all my ingredients and got going.

It looks so easy in the book. All you do is rub a bit of butter into some flour with a pinch of salt, slosh in a bit of milk and roll it out. Abracadabra – scones! Yeah, right. On another planet maybe. Meanwhile, here is the Alex Bond account of how to make scones:

1. Tear the bag of flour so that it spills open and covers you head to toe in white dust.
2. Put what flour you can scrape off into the bowl with a whole ton of salt because the top comes off the saltcellar.
3. Fish out the top of the saltcellar and spray a bit more flour around the place.

4. Add too much milk because it keeps sloshing over the side of the tablespoon when you're measuring it.
5. Add more flour to soak up the extra milk.
6. Try to add more butter because you've got too much flour and milk.
7. When your scone dough has all the lumps and bumps you can bear to look at, dump it in the bin and start again.

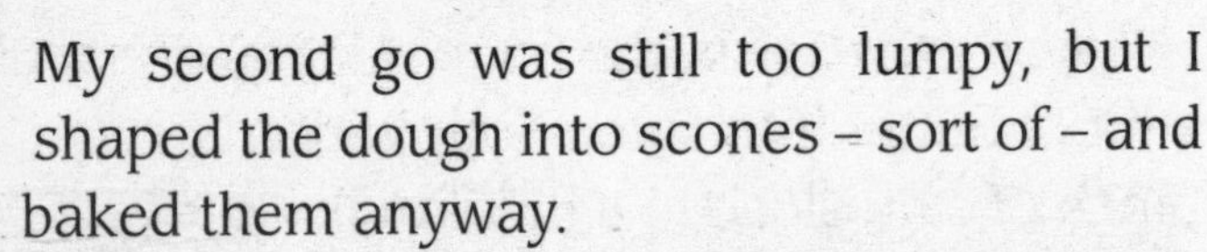

My second go was still too lumpy, but I shaped the dough into scones – sort of – and baked them anyway.

They came out a bit harder than I'd expected. But Bear loved them! So having passed the first test, I offered one to everyone else.

'No thanks, love. I'm still full from dinner,' said Mum, glaring at Dad who was now chomping his way through a ham sandwich.

Dad took a look at Batch Two then quickly held up his sandwich. 'Maybe I'll have a try at Batch Three,' he said.

Evan was more brutal. 'They look disgustin',' he said. 'Scones shouldn't be all lumpy an' hard.'

'Bear loves them,' I defended.

'Bear prob'ly thinks they're dog biscuits,' Evan replied.

I gave Evan a 'look'. But I could see what he meant.

I wasn't going to give up though. I set my alarm clock to get up early the next morning – quite a sacrifice, as I love to sleep in on a Saturday and then read in bed for a while. But I was determined.

Alex never gave up during those early attempts at her exclusive Alex Bond Designer Scone recipe. It was that grit and determination that took her to being one of the top-ten celebrities on TV today . . .

So, on Saturday morning, I had another go.

Or three.

By lunchtime, I'd covered all three of Mum's cooling racks with . . . well, the first was a batch of knobbly golden lumps, and the second a batch of smooth burnt lumps. But on the

third baking rack, were proper, round, golden-brown scones. I'd cracked it!

Mum and Dad and even Evan ate one. And they all said they'd be a 'taster panel' for me when I tried adding my mysterious and exotic flavours to the mix the following day. Rosie agreed to be on the taster panel too and said she'd try to persuade her big brother, Josh, to come round as well. Josh is really cool and we thought it would be good to have his opinion.

On Sunday morning I began adding different flavours to bits of scone dough.

Evan made very loud vomiting sounds at my very first attempt: cheese, maple syrup and fennel seeds – so I expelled him from the panel.

The others tasters were a bit more polite, although everyone agreed that there was no hope for that particular flavour combination. Even Bear seemed to have trouble swallowing it. Then he went to his water bowl and drained it dry. But at least he didn't start wiping his mouth along the kitchen rug this time.

By the seventh unsuccessful flavour

combination, my taster panel was looking a bit fed-up.

'Um, could I have a glass of water, please?' Josh asked.

'Get one of the more poisonous ones, Josh?' asked Dad.

'Da-ad!' I was really hurt. I knew they were disgusting – but it's a bit much when even your own parents are honest and unbiased.

'If you're going to be a famous cook, you'll hear worse than that from food critics in the newspapers, Alex,' Dad said. 'And remember, your namesake, Alexander the Great, overcame many more hurdles than this to make his name.'

Very inspiring, I'm sure. Most of Alexander the Great's hurdles were overcome by going to war with people – not much of an option in a cookery contest.

Dad'll be sorry one day when a big newspaper really is interviewing me.

'So, Alex, did your family support you?'

'My mother did her best, but I'm afraid my father was quite scathing about my early attempts.' Alex gave a little laugh and tossed her head defiantly, showing some of the grit and determination that has made her one of the

greatest chefs of our times. 'He was right, of course: some of those early creations were quite disgusting. But I know Dad now regrets not being more supportive. He just didn't believe world-championship class was within my grasp . . .'

Josh suddenly remembered that he had some urgent homework to do and rushed off home. Rosie rolled her eyes.

I finally did it on the ninth try. Cheese, chopped dates and cardamom. Everyone liked it and looked very relieved that they did.

'They've got a nice smell,' Evan said. I decided to let him back on the panel. 'They taste OK too,' he said, taking another bite.

'You'll have to think of a good name for them,' said Rosie.

Evan stuffed the rest of his scone in his mouth in one go. 'Yeah,' he agreed, spraying crumbs all over me. But for once I didn't mind too much. 'Why don't you call them "Nice Smelly Cakes"?' he suggested.

'Don't be silly,' I said. 'That sounds like old socks. Dad, can you think of a name? Maybe a French one, like before?'

'*Gateaux Aromatiques*,' said Dad. 'French for aromatic cakes,' he translated. 'Aromatic means smelly, but in a nice way. Nothing to do with socks.'

I liked it. It sounded posh and a bit exotic. The kind of name a famous chef might give her own brand-new creation. 'Good one, Dad. Thanks!' I said.

'You're welcome,' he replied. 'Now, if I'm not mistaken, the next thing we'll be eating is Sunday lunch . . .'

'Is that a hint?' Mum asked, smiling. 'Well, I'm cooking something a bit special today: pork stuffed with prunes, served with char-grilled honeyed vegetables and –'

'Chips?' asked Evan.

'– sautéed garlic potato diamonds,' finished Mum.

Evan glowered and climbed on to Dad's lap. He doesn't do this much now as he's decided that being five means he's all grown-up.

Then Dad said, 'No.'

'No what?' Mum asked.

'No pruned pork with chargrilled this and garlicky that. No more Will Masters. It's all lovely, Julie, but it's too much. It's like having Christmas dinner every day. How about we save the pruney pork for another time and just have cheese on toast?'

'Or sausage and chips?' said Evan.

'Yes! Sausage and chips!' repeated Dad. 'And I'll cook it.'

So that's what we had. And I shared my last sausage with Bear, so he loved me again.

Now I had the recipe, it was a matter of fine-tuning and practising. I slaved every night the following week (fortunately, Mum's cooking phase was over, so I had the kitchen to myself). But, by Friday evening, Mum, Dad and Evan refused to eat any more. They said they'd done their bit; enough was enough. I looked round at the plates heaped with *Gateaux Aromatiques*. I decided to freeze a couple of platefuls. They'd change their minds after I won the competition. But that still left loads.

Then I had an inspired idea. I tore off squares of kitchen roll – not that there was much of it left, as I'd used most of it on kitchen accidents – and wrapped the *Gateaux Aromatiques* into little parcels. I delivered a little parcel to each doorstep in our neighbourhood. I imagined the surprise and delight of all our friends and neighbours when they found their free samples of my soon-to-be famous Designer Scone.

'Alex was always an imaginative and generous little girl,' smiled Julie Bond, her mother, remembering. 'Her first success – the Gateaux Aromatiques, *which have gone into Alex Bond legend – are still a talking point after all these years. What happened was . . .'*

The next morning, Mum came in from pegging out the washing with a strange look on her face.

'What's the matter?' asked Dad.

'Maggie next door's just asked me if we got a little food parcel on our front doorstep this morning,' Mum told him. 'It seems everyone else in the street got one. So I'm just going to open the front door and have a look.'

I grinned proudly and was just about to explain.

But then Mum added, 'Probably someone with a grudge according to Gavin over the road. He's seen it all before, being a policeman. He says it encourages vermin – mice, even rats! Maggie hates mice. She saw one sniffing about when she went to put out her milk bottles. She jumped right into her pansies. Squashed them flat! It's just pure malice.'

Dad looked incredulous. 'Who on earth would –?'

Mum and Dad both jumped to the same conclusion at the same moment. They turned their heads like a couple of perfectly synchronized robots and stared at me.

'Got to go,' I said. 'Promised to meet Rosie. Bye!' I legged it down the path as fast as my legs would carry me.

How we suffer for our art.

Chapter Six

I didn't sleep much the night before the competition. As soon as it was light, I got up and started packing my ingredients. But Bear thought I was going away and started barking his disapproval, which woke everyone up.

They were all OK about it, though. Even Evan the Terrible was a bit nicer than usual.

'I hope you win,' he said.

'Thanks,' I said, surprised. Maybe my little brother wasn't so terrible.

'Cos Dad says he'll take us all to Ben's Burger Bar if you do,' Evan added, as he buried his snout back into his cornflakes.

And then again, maybe he was.

Dad kissed me and ruffled the hair that I had

just finished trying to plait. 'Knock 'em dead, kiddo. Literally, if that's what it takes to win.'

'Martin!' Mum looked very disapproving.

Dad winked at me. 'Your mother will fill your head with all this nonsense about it being the taking part that's important. But you and I know it's about winning, so you keep an eye on that Pearl Barconi. Take her out if you have to –'

'Martin, Evan is listening!' Mum was using her stern no-nonsense voice now.

Dad knew it was time to quit while he was still ahead. 'Break a leg, Alex!' he called, then he scarpered into his study.

'Why does Dad want Alex to break a leg?' asked Evan.

'He doesn't really,' Mum told him. 'It's just something people say. It's a superstition that if you say the worst, then the worst won't happen.'

'That's silly,' said Evan immediately, 'because it would be even worse to break your back, or both arms. Why don't they say, "Break your arms" or "Break your back"?'

'It's just a *saying*, Evan!' I said.

Mum was going to walk up to Barconi's with me on her way to work, but I suddenly realized something. Usually Mum wore her uniform to work. Today she was dressed in her smart trousers and new boots and a shirt she usually wore for going out in the evening. 'Mum, why aren't you wearing your uniform?' I asked suspiciously.

'I just fancied a change,' she said airily. 'I'll put on my uniform when I get to the hospital.' But she was blushing.

'You're hoping to see Will, aren't you?' I accused her. 'Mum, don't be embarrassing.'

'I don't know what you mean, Alex,' she sniffed.

There was no time to argue. Evan's friend and his mum were at the door, waiting to take Evan to school, and we still had to get out of the house, past Bear.

He knew something was going on. I lured him into the garden with a sausage while Mum put the bags outside the front door.

'Ready!' she yelled, and I rushed back into the house, slamming the back door behind me so that Bear couldn't follow. He was barking like mad.

'He'll be fine in a minute,' said Mum.

Sure enough, by the time we were three

houses down, Bear had gone quiet. Feeling a bit guilty, I pictured him slumped miserably against the back door, waiting for our return.

As we got close to the restaurant we could see the *What's Cooking, Will?* trailer, and the film crew dashing around with cables and trolleys.

'They're here already,' said Mum excitedly.

'Here, let me help with that,' said a cheerful voice behind us.

Mum gasped as Will Masters offered to take the bag of ingredients from her.

'Thank you,' she said. 'You're . . . you're Will Masters.'

'Yes, I know,' he said. He came close and lowered his voice, as though he was sharing a deep secret. 'To be honest, I've known for some time.'

Mum blushed, and then she giggled. It was *so* embarrassing!

Will led the way to the kitchen. 'Let's go and find you a working space,' he said over his shoulder.

Mum began to follow him.

I stopped her. 'No, Mum, not you!' I said. 'Will means *me*! You've got to go to work, remember?'

'Ah yes. Well, um . . . I was just going to tell Will how well his Oriental Chicken Parcels turned out.' She caught my eye. 'But I don't want to be late for work. So, bye then, love. Have fun, and don't worry about winning, because –'

'It's the taking part that matters,' I finished. 'Yes, Mum. Look, I've got to go. Bye.'

I took off after Will before Mum could launch into her pep talk about how bad it was to be too competitive.

The kitchen was huge. Most of it seemed to be made of shining stainless steel and there were loads of spotlights built into the ceiling, which made the room really bright. There were people everywhere. Kids were taking things out of bags and collecting bits of equipment; chefs and waiters in Barconi uniforms were watching and helping. Miss Westrop was walking around – in another new dress. The camera crew were setting up lights and moving camera trolleys around. The noise and bustle were amazing. I started getting butterflies.

'Good morning, good morning!' Amber Barconi was fluttering about, dressed like a film star. Mr Barconi was there too, standing quietly in the background. He was watching his wife and shaking his head, as if he didn't understand her at all. I don't blame him.

Amber fluttered over to me. 'Alison, isn't it?' she gushed. 'Pearl talks about you all the time.'

'Alex,' I corrected, forcing a polite smile.

'Yes, of course. Got everything you need, have you? Good.'

Before I had time to draw breath, never mind answer the question, she was talking to someone else.

Will grinned at me. I got the feeling he found Amber as much of a pain as I did. 'Here you go,' he said. 'Next to Rosie. Will that do?'

'Hiya,' said Rosie.

'Oh, yeah, thanks!' I gave him a relieved smile. 'That's great. We're best friends!' I sounded all blubbery because I was nervous.

'I know,' Will confessed. 'Rosie told me. And don't be nervous. Just get your ingredients ready. Everybody has to stop cooking at twelve o'clock for the judging, but you've plenty of time. Ignore the cameras as much as you can. We're here to have fun, yeah?' He patted my arm, and moved away to talk to a cameraman.

'Will's *so* great,' said Rosie happily. 'He saw

me looking for you and said he'd keep the place next to me free until you arrived.'

I agreed Will was great and began to unpack my stuff. I was halfway through when I heard a dog barking.

A big dog, probably something like a Newfoundland.

Bear, in fact.

'Alex,' Rosie said, 'is that . . . did you remember to lock the garden gate?'

There it was again. 'Woof.'

'Oh no!' I wailed, my heart sinking into my trainers. I pictured myself slamming the back door to stop Bear following me in. But I hadn't checked that the gate on to the street was locked. And Bear knows how to lever it open.

I hurried out into the yard behind the restaurant. Bear was waiting there for me. He was very happy to see me, jumping around and chasing his tail in a circle. Finally, he launched himself at me and nearly knocked me over.

'What is that *dog* doing here?'

I turned to see Amber standing in the doorway. She was eyeing Bear distastefully, following the trail of dribble from his huge jaws to her potted plants on the patio.

'Sorry,' I muttered. 'He managed to open the gate somehow, and he's followed me. I'll . . . I'll take him home.'

'No time.' Will had come to investigate and heard what I'd said. 'Amber, couldn't we just tie him up for now? He can't do any harm out here.'

I wasn't too convinced about that, but I didn't want to leave the competition.

Amber hesitated. I could tell she wanted to say no, but she didn't want to disagree with her famous guest. Finally, she sighed. 'Very well, Alison. Tie him to the drainpipe.'

'Alex,' I said.

'Yes,' she said impatiently. 'Tie Alex to the drainpipe. Now, excuse me, I must get on.' She wafted back into the restaurant.

'Good luck, Alex,' said Will, winking at me. He followed Amber inside.

But as soon as I tried to go in, Bear started barking again.

'Shut that dog up!' yelled a sound engineer.

I hurried back over to Bear. 'Quiet, Bear!' I said fiercely.

Bear stopped barking. He could tell I was serious.

'Bear, you are a pain and if you muck this up

for me I might never forgive you,' I went on sternly. 'So you've got to lie down right there.'

Bear followed my finger and then he slumped down on the ground where I'd pointed.

'And you stay there until I come back for you,' I added. 'Or there'll be big trouble. Understand?' Of course, he didn't understand the words. But he understood the tone of my voice.

He put his head on his paws and looked up at me with such sorrowful brown eyes that I felt really bad.

'Good boy, Bear.' I patted his head and he wagged his tail a bit. 'I'll be back as soon as I can. Promise.'

He didn't bark when I left him this time. I waited inside the door where he couldn't see me for a couple of minutes to make sure he settled.

Silence.

I breathed a sigh of relief. Then I poked my head round the door very carefully so he wouldn't see me.

I needn't have worried. Bear had found a new distraction. The rope I had tied him with was long enough to let him reach the small herb garden growing beside the patio. He was steadily sampling all the herbs. He seemed to like them. *At least he'll have minty-fresh breath*, I thought.

I went back into the kitchen. It was time to start cooking.

Chapter Seven

When I got back to my place I could see straight away that Rosie was annoyed.

'What's up?' I asked.

As if in answer, Pearl appeared at my elbow. She looked over my ingredients and smiled. 'Ah, something not too ambitious by the look of it. Very wise. And Rosie's doing a pudding, of course. Clearly, her favourite thing.'

Rosie, who is very sensitive about being a tiny bit plump, went even redder.

Pearl turned to a passing cameraman. 'Everything all right? Can we, at Barconi's, do anything to assist you?' she asked, as if she owned the place.

'Oh, I think we can manage, thank you,' said the cameraman. He raised his eyebrows at one of the chefs as Pearl turned back to us.

'We don't need any help either, Macaroni,' I said, trying to sound like Miss Westrop does when she wants you to go away.

But Pearl didn't budge. 'So, Alex, what *are* you cooking?' she asked nosily.

I drew myself up to look tall and proud and put on my best French accent. '*Gateaux Aromatiques*,' I said. 'My own recipe, of course.'

That stumped her. 'Mmm.' I could see she was trying to translate, but couldn't. 'Very . . . nice,' she said finally.

'Pearl, haven't you got to get your own stuff ready?' asked Rosie.

I knew as soon as Rosie opened her mouth that she was playing right into Macaroni's hands – she was just waiting for a chance to talk about her own dish – but my well-aimed kick didn't get to Rosie in time.

'Oh, I've done all *my* preparation,' Pearl replied, batting her eyelashes and pretending to look modest. 'I've kept things simple. We Barconis are very big on simple food.'

And simple minds, I thought. But I managed to keep my mouth shut.

'The pasta is resting, and the machine is oiled and ready to roll,' Pearl went on.

'I shall be making ravioli – parcels of pasta –'

'We know what ravioli is, Macaroni,' said Rosie.

'Ah, ravioli,' said Will, coming up with the camera crew. 'One of the classic Italian dishes, eh, Pearl?'

Pearl's eyelashes went into overdrive; she was batting them so hard she could have taken off any minute. 'Ah, but *proper* Italian ravioli is very different. I know all about pasta. My Italian grandpa made a fortune selling it, you know,' she simpered. 'I shall be filling *my* ravioli with a paste of sun-dried tomatoes, lightly spiced with chilli. She smiled straight into the camera. 'Grandpa sends us the best chillis and olive oil from Italy. Just a tiny amount of his chilli gives quite a kick!'.

'I'd like to give *you* a kick,' I murmured.

Pearl gave me a 'look' and carried on. 'I shall drizzle the ravioli with some of Grandpa's olive oil, flavoured with basil – fresh from Mummy's garden.'

'What's all that other stuff for?' asked Rosie,

nodding across to where Pearl's ingredients lay. There was a pile of lemons and a bag of icing sugar.

Pearl tossed her dark glossy hair for the camera and said lightly, 'Oh, that's just to keep me occupied once I've finished, while everyone catches up. Iced lemon balls are a perfect dessert to follow ravioli. It's Papa's own recipe, a closely guarded secret, so don't ask me about it.' She paused, waiting for someone to ask her about it.

But no one did.

'Fair enough,' Will said, then he turned to the cameraman. 'Over there next,' he instructed and they hurried off.

Looking a bit put out, Macaroni went back to her place.

As I started taking the stones out of my dates, Will and Amber came and stood near to me and Rosie.

'And this is Amber Barconi, who is generously hosting this event,' Will said into the camera. 'Why did you want to get involved, Amber?' he asked.

She could hardly say, 'Because I was desperate to be on the telly', could she? But I was sure that, like Macaroni, Amber wouldn't pass

by the opportunity to show off. And she didn't disappoint . . .

'Well, Will . . .' Amber purred, 'as a former model, I know only too well the pitfalls of today's junk-food diet. So I have come to realize how important it is to pass on my cooking skills to my daughter, Pearl – who is here today, cooking a Barconi recipe.' She gave a little wave to Pearl, who batted her eyelashes back and smiled at the camera. 'Pearl is using only the best of Barconi ingredients – just as we do here in the restaurant. And she is cooking just one of the Barconi dishes that can be ordered through Amber Nectar, my upmarket party-food company –'

'Yes, thanks,' Will interrupted hurriedly. He obviously thought she'd had enough free advertising.

I caught a glimpse of Mr Barconi hovering in the background. He was holding his head in his hands. He looked like he thought Amber had said enough too.

But Amber wasn't done yet. She leaned out and put her hand on my shoulder. 'And as a thank you to the lovely children like Alice here, who have come to promote the love of fresh food with Barconi's Italian Restaurant, we will be treating every one of them to a special Barconi ice-cream sundae.' She looked down at Rosie and me. 'Even the losers. Barconi's ice-cream sundaes are our speciality. The taste of real Italy –'

She would have gone on, but Will cut her short and the camera panned to the happy faces who had cheered at the mention of free food.

And so it was that I got to be standing next to Will Masters, celebrity chef, close up on TV for what seemed like ages. I'm glad I was able to enjoy the moment. I'm glad I didn't know at the time that I'd dribbled toothpaste on to my T-shirt that morning.

Chapter Eight

Everyone settled down to concentrate on their recipes. I went to turn on the oven. It looked like something from another planet, or *Star Wars*. I was used to Mum's gas oven. But this oven was electric, with a fan thing that made a loud noise when you turned it on.

'Having trouble?'

I looked round. One of the chefs was standing by me.

'I'm Karim,' he said. 'Do you need a hand?'

'Um, I'm Alex,' I muttered. 'And I don't know how to turn on the oven.' My face was hot; I felt so stupid.

'Don't worry,' said Karim kindly. 'These ovens are a bit complicated. Show me your recipe and I'll work out the right temperature.'

I handed over my scruffy notes.

'Mmm. Interesting combination of flavours. Old family recipe, is it?' Karim asked.

'No, it's mine,' I said.

Karim smiled. 'A real cook.' He looked sideways at Amber, who was still twittering away in the background. 'Maybe you could tell Amber Barconi how it's done.'

'But she cooks for the stars!' I said.

Karim snorted. He leaned towards me and murmured in my ear, 'You didn't hear this from me, but Amber Barconi doesn't know one end of a zabaglione from another. We do all her cooking. She gets all the credit.'

'You're kidding,' I said. I looked over at Rosie, but she was busy cooking, and hadn't heard.

'Like I say, you didn't hear it from me,' said Karim. 'Now, let's sort out this oven.'

I was bursting to tell Rosie Amber's dark secret, but time was ticking away and I had to finish making my *Gateaux Aromatiques*. When I'd finished I put the tray in the oven, crossed my fingers and my toes and my eyes, and wished for luck.

'A real cook,' Karim had said. I decided that when I was famous – too famous to do much cooking – I would have Karim as my head chef. I had a feeling that he would be happy to leave Barconi's.

I started planning my restaurant. Dad was always calling me Alexandra the Great, so why not use it as a theme? We could have ancient Greek statues and pillars. All the stars would come for my opening night. Mum and Dad would be guests of honour. And Evan, maybe, if he swore a solemn vow not to be pointlessly embarrassing. The menus would be really classy . . .

'Hey, Alex – what do you think?'

It was Rosie. Her pudding was out of the oven and she was starting on the sauce.

'It's looking great, Rosie,' I said. 'Will you give me a taste, afterwards?'

She nodded and looked around with a puzzled expression on her face. 'What's that smell?' she hissed.

'What smell?' I sniffed the air. There was a definite whiff of burning in the air – and it was coming from my oven! A little wisp of smoke floated upwards.

'Oh no!' I heard Amber wail. 'Whose oven is that? It'll set off the –'

I couldn't hear what she said next because an almighty clanging of bells drowned everything else out.

'Right, Class Six. Just stand still a moment and don't panic,' yelled Miss Westrop.

She looked at Amber, waiting for instructions. Were we going to have to do a fire drill?

Amber made a dash for the alarm box mounted on the wall and jabbed at the controls. The bells stopped. 'It's OK,' she said, tight-lipped but trying to smile because the camera was there. 'It's just the smoke alarm. We have them above the ovens as an early-warning system.'

She turned to the camera, her smile a bit more composed now the noise had stopped. 'Here at Barconi's we are very safety conscious. Our chefs are very highly skilled – usually –' she glared at me – 'they do not leave things to burn.'

'Oh, I don't know,' said Will easily. 'I've burned a few things in my time, haven't you, Amber?'

'I . . . er . . .' Amber looked confused and two of the chefs sniggered.

I knew why – because those manicured nails of hers had never been near a baking tray!

'OK, Alex, let's survey the damage, eh?' said Will kindly.

The camera moved in for a close-up and I

stood rooted to the spot, my cheeks burning hotter than the oven. Behind Will, I could see Macaroni trying to look shocked and sympathetic. She had her hand to her mouth, but I knew she was smirking.

Will gently moved me aside and opened the oven door. Smoke billowed out and he coughed. 'Oh dear,' he said, and held up the tray so the camera could get a good shot.

The tops of my *Gateaux*, which were supposed to be all golden, were black and smoking.

'Oh, Alex,' said Will. When he saw I was trying not to cry, he waved the cameras away. 'Are you all right?' he asked.

I nodded, but I couldn't say anything.

'Don't worry about it. These things happen,' he said. He moved on after the cameras. I wished I could summon up a bigger puff of smoke and disappear in it.

A sea of sympathetic faces surrounded me. Rosie looked almost as upset as me. 'I'm OK, honestly,' I said. 'But I'd better check on Bear.' I stumbled out, glad of the excuse for leaving.

Bear was out in the yard where I had left him. Well, almost where I had left him.

The herb garden was pretty much demolished and Bear had now turned his attention to a white van that had backed into the yard. 'Amber Nectar' was painted in big gold letters on the side. It guessed it must be Amber's delivery van, waiting to be loaded with food Karim and the other chefs had made for Amber to pass off as her own.

Someone hadn't shut the rear door properly. Bear could just about reach it from his rope and had managed to pull the door open. He was happily munching his way through the nearest tray of food.

'Bear! No!' I wailed. I snatched the tray away. There was one piece of food left on it. A savoury tart, about the size of a scone – filled with something dark green – something spinachy, maybe. The label and delivery note on the tray said *'Hand-cooked especially for you by Amber Nectar.'*

I wanted to go and hide somewhere and have a good old cry. But then I looked at Bear. He stared at me with his big trusting eyes. He clearly thought I was going to do something more useful. Like save his behind.

'Come on Alex, think!' I said to myself.

I thought.

And then I went swiftly into action to try and disguise Bear's vandalism. I dashed back inside and grabbed my poor burned *Gateaux*. Then I arranged them on the Amber Nectar tray. I looked at the remaining green tart, then shrugged, and threw it over to Bear who caught and swallowed it in one smooth action.

Next, I hastily picked all the green leaves from the corner of the herb garden Bear hadn't been able to reach. I squashed them on top of the *Gateaux*, then stood back to look at my handiwork.

Not bad.

Then I stuffed the tray back in the van and slammed the door shut properly.

'Now, lie down, Bear!' I said.

Bear lay down.

'Good boy,' I said, and he thumped his tail. 'And you must *stay* now until I come back and get you. No more eating, OK?' I wagged a warning finger at him.

He closed his eyes, pretending not to notice.

'Alex, are you OK?'

I whirled round, face like beetroot, freckles on full alert.

It was Will. 'I'm so sorry about your dish,

Alex. If it's any comfort at all, it made fabulous TV, and you'll be tugging on everyone's heart-strings when the programme goes out. You'll be the talk of the nation.'

'Yeah, great,' I said. My big chance to be on TV and it had to be as the girl who nearly set the restaurant alight. I'd blown my chance to be a famous chef, but I was definitely in the running to be a famous clown . . .

Chapter Nine

Rosie was just mixing her fizzy sauce. At least things were going right for her.

'Are you all right?' she asked.

'Not really,' I said. I told her about Bear and what I'd done.

Rosie laughed, and whisked her sauce furiously. 'You are amazing, Alex. You're such a quick thinker. I wouldn't have had the faintest idea what to do. But you always manage to come up with a brilliant idea when you most need one.'

If only that were true, I thought. And then it happened, just like Rosie said. A brilliant idea popped straight into my head. A brilliant, world-famous-cook type of idea.

I flew at Rosie like a demented thing. 'Quick, what have you got left?' I asked her.

'Eh? What?' she said, startled.

'I'm going to have a crack at Alaska Surprise.'

The great thing about being friends with Rosie is that we know each other so well, we never have to bother with lengthy explanations. Rosie immediately held out half a pack of butter and a bowl with a couple of spoonfuls of jam left in the bottom.

'I've got a couple of spare eggs somewhere too,' she said.

'OK, so we have butter, eggs, jam – I still need bread and ice cream,' I said.

Rosie shook her head. 'Sorry, haven't got either.'

'Ten minutes left,' called Will. He was looking over at us curiously. I hoped he wouldn't think there was something worth investigating going on.

I looked around wildly. No one seemed to be using bread. But over on the other side of the kitchen Karim was preparing the ice-cream sundaes.

I dashed across. 'Hi, Karim, no time to explain, but can I have my sundae now, rather than later, please?'

Karim handed me a sundae right away. 'What are you up to?' he asked curiously.

'You'll see in a minute – if I manage to find some bread. Thanks.' I ran off.

I fished the chunks of fruit out of the sundae. The strawberry syrup and chopped nuts would have to stay. Still no bread. It was so frustrating. I racked my brains to think of what I could use instead. But there wasn't really anything.

'It's no good,' I said miserably. 'I can't do it. I need at least two slices of bread.'

'There you go!' Karim handed me a little plate of sandwiches. 'We prepared sandwiches for everybody to eat at lunchtime,' he explained.

'Tell me they're not peanut butter,' I said, holding by breath.

Karim smiled. 'I chose the easiest ones. Salad and just a tiny bit of mayonnaise. Got to go now. Good luck.'

'Thanks, Karim!' I called.

I put Rosie's butter in a large frying pan to heat and whipped up the eggs with some milk in a bowl. At home there would be cinnamon and nutmeg to hand, but there was no time to search for them here. I hoped the extra flavour of the syrup and nuts from the sundae would make up for it.

Carefully I scraped off what I could from the sandwich and dipped the bread into the egg mixture.

'Five minutes, guys!' called Will.

Just enough time. I looked up quickly and saw Karim talking to Will. He was pointing at me.

'Oh no,' I groaned to Rosie. 'I think I'm going to be disqualified. Maybe you're not allowed to have two goes.'

'And maybe you *are* allowed,' said Rosie sensibly. 'So until you know, just get on with it. You've got nothing to lose now.'

Into the frying pan. This was the crucial bit. I needed to have the sandwich complete before time was up, but not so much before that the ice cream would melt. I watched the clock carefully. After two minutes, I flipped over the bread and got ready with a plate.

With one minute to go I took the bread out of the pan and spread each slice with jam straight away. Then I emptied the sundae out of the glass on to one of the slices and stuck the second slice on top.

There were two or three green flecks of lettuce that hadn't come away. They made the bread look a bit mouldy.

'Rosie, can I have your leftover icing sugar?' I asked.

'Oh, sorry, Alex,' she said. 'I used it all.' Rosie looked at my Alaska Surprise. 'Mmm. I can see why you might need it. But wait up! Pearl has icing sugar . . .'

'Yeah,' I said. 'And of course she'll be dying to share it with me so that I can try and win instead of her.'

'But didn't you hear what Miss Westrop said?' Rosie smiled. 'It's the taking part that counts. Besides, I wasn't planning to ask her . . . stay here.'

Rosie marched straight over to Pearl's working space, lifted the icing sugar and walked back. Not a single person seemed to notice or, if they did, no one was going to tell.

I covered the whole plate in icing sugar, and it made a sort of skirt round the sandwich. It looked so pretty I decided to make it a permanent feature of the recipe from now on.

'Time's up!' called Will. Everyone cheered and clapped.

Will smiled into the camera. 'Wow! I don't know about you, but I've been feeling as nervous as any of these kids. What a talented lot you are, Derrington Primary School. I can't wait to try all the food. And what about poor old Alex?'

Suddenly the camera was on me. I felt like a stunned rabbit.

'Well,' Will continued, 'a little bird has told me that Alex has made a remarkable recovery from her earlier disaster. Tune in after the break to find out how!' He pointed at the camera, smiled, and the camera moved away.

'OK, hold your places, guys!' he said. 'We're not really having the break now, that's just for recording purposes. On with the judging! Alex, we're going to come to you first, before that melts.' He grinned. 'You're a trooper, Alex. Real star quality. Well done.'

I felt so good I could swear that even my freckles twinkled.

'I'm going to ask you a couple of questions, and then taste your, er . . .'

'Alaska Surprise,' I said helpfully.

'Yeah, that too. Right, cameras ready?'

The producer nodded and Will began. 'Remember the disaster in part one, where young Alexandra Bond's recipe went up in flames? Well, let me tell you that this young lady has the stuff of true greatness in her. Undaunted, she started again – and came up with a completely different recipe, made on the hoof. Tell us about it, Alex.'

'It's something I do a lot at home,' I said. 'It's very easy and quick, but it tastes really great. Even my little brother likes it and he's a really picky eater.'

'Well, let's see if we agree with your brother. On to the judging,' said Will with a huge, gorgeous smile.

This was it. The moment of truth. My last-minute Alaska Surprise was unlikely to win, but would it be enough to save me from the embarrassment of coming last? I was about to find out.

Chapter Ten

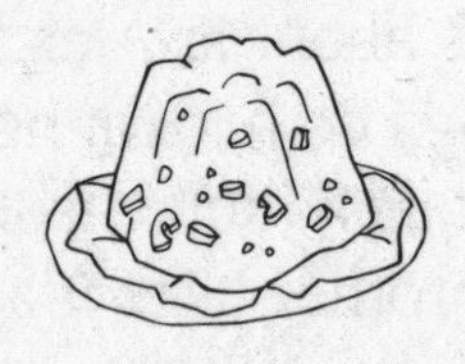

Will got his testing spoon and took a mouthful of my Alaska Surprise. 'Mmm,' he said. 'It's very unusual. You can still feel the warmth of the French toast but the coldness of the ice cream cuts across the palate before the soothing jam – or is it syrup? – trickles across your tongue. Mmm. Slightly tangy –' (That will be the mayonnaise from the sandwich, I thought) – 'and yet deliciously sweet. Well done, Alex.'

Rosie gave me a thumbs up and then turned pale as Will moved on to her Fizzy Apricot Pudding.

'Lovely colour,' Will enthused. He cut a small slice and poured on some of the sauce. 'Ooh, it's fizzy,' he said. 'Fizzy apricots! An inspired idea. Well done, Rosie.'

He moved on down the line and Rosie and I

hugged each other. Will Masters had said 'Well done!' We were going to be on the telly! OK, maybe I had blown my chances of winning and becoming Alexandra the Great Chef, but it would be practice for the day I *did* become famous.

Meanwhile, Will had reached Joe Mackey's creation. I could just see it from my position. I think it was some kind of trifle, but the cream on top was dark grey, and the Smarties Joe had stuck on top had started to leak colour all over it.

Will looked at the trifle thoughtfully. 'Bit of a problem with the Smarties, Joe?'

Joe nodded miserably.

'I had that problem myself once,' said Will. 'But it's the taste that counts, eh?'

Joe brightened a bit and leaned forward intensely to watch Will eat.

As the spoon went to his mouth, a lump fell out of the custard. Will chewed slowly. His mouth sort of twisted and no one saw him swallow.

'Well, Joe, that's a very, um, interesting trifle. The custard is actually quite chunky, isn't it?'

Joe nodded. 'That's right. It's the way my mum always does it.'

'Mmm, yes. And the – cream is it? Unusual colour.'

'Liquorice,' said Joe promptly.

'Right. Well, a unique touch. Good work, Joe.'

Very quietly, Will's assistant handed him a glass of water and a napkin and he moved on.

I couldn't see what was going on for the next couple of contestants. It was a good job my Alaska Surprise had been judged first. It was beginning to look a sorry sight as the ice cream melted. I took a bite. It still tasted good though.

Rosie leaned over and pinched the spoon. 'Let's have some. Oh yes. You haven't lost your touch, Miss Bond.'

'And your Fizzy Apricot Pud is highly commendable, Miss Stevens.'

We giggled.

'Do be quiet, you two,' said Pearl bossily. 'Will is still judging!'

We pulled faces at her, but we stopped talking.

'What have we here?' Will asked.

'Savoury salad,' said Felicity.

It was a slab of green jelly resting on a bed of lettuce. Inside the jelly you could see little cubes of what looked like carrot and other stuff that could have been anything.

'Unusual,' murmured Will. 'I've seen things like this in the United States. Quite eye-catching.'

He took a spoonful. 'Ah-hah. Carrot, a bit of celery. And –' His expression changed, and he chewed a bit. The assistant hovered with the water and the napkin, but Will recovered and swallowed quickly. 'I don't know what that was, but it tasted – well, meaty.'

'Sausages,' said Felicity. 'We had some left over one day, and I just had this idea of cutting them up with the other leftovers and putting them in a jelly. We eat it on birthdays, when people come round, or sometimes at Christmas.'

'Yes, it's definitely not an everyday food,' said Will. 'Well done, Felicity. And now, last but not least, Pearl. What do you have for us, Pearl?'

Pearl batted her eyelashes at the camera and took a deep breath. 'Ravioli stuffed with sun-dried tomatoes and a hint of chilli, then drizzled with basil-infused olive oil,' she said.

'Right then,' said Will, 'let's give it a try.' He took a piece of ravioli, swirled it in the sauce and popped it into his mouth.

What happened next is a bit of a blur, which is a pity, because I'd love to be able to remember it properly.

No sooner was the ravioli in his mouth than Will gave a strangled scream and spat it out again. He didn't even wait for the napkin. 'Aaagh!' he gasped, pointing at the plate and at his throat.

'What? What is it? Speak to me, Will!' shouted Amber.

But he didn't seem able to.

Everybody crowded in.

Will stared wildly all around him. 'Hot! Hot!' he gasped, waving his hands in front of his mouth. Without thinking, I grabbed my Alaska Surprise and shoved it into his hands. Ice cream immediately started to ooze over his fingers.

'Cold! Cold!' I shouted.

With both hands, Will crammed the remains of my Alaska Surprise into his mouth.

'Oh no!' A sudden wail from Amber made us

all turn away from Will. 'Pearl Barconi, what have you done?'

Amber's face was like thunder and in her hands she had two small bowls of red stuff. At first they looked the same to me, but then I noticed that one of them was a bit brighter red and a bit smoother.

'Pearl, which one of these did you stuff the ravioli with?' demanded Amber.

Pearl looked confused. 'The sun-dried tomato one, of course.' She peered at the bowls and pointed to one of them. 'That one. The tomatoes.'

Amber shrieked. 'That's the *chillies.* You've given Will Masters a whole mouthful of extra-strong *chillies*! Pearl, how could you?'

Amber ran to the drinking tap and started filling a huge jug with water. 'Benito, get some ice!' she snapped to a waiter. 'His mouth will be on fire for hours.'

Pearl stood rooted to the spot. 'You should have *told* me,' she snapped to her mother. 'You were watching every move I made. Why didn't *you* notice, Mother? It's not *my* fault.'

I almost felt sorry for Pearl Barconi. My sympathy lasted about a second and a half. I was actually on my way over to say something nice to her when the camera came towards us. Pearl thought I was going to hog her shot, so she shoved me out of the way. She looked straight into the camera with a tragic heroine expression. 'I didn't realize . . .' she said to the camera, her bottom lip wobbling. 'Can he ever forgive me?'

The cameraman snorted – I think it was a laugh, but he tried to make it into a sneeze – and swung away. It was the same old Macaroni, after all.

Will drank a whole jugful of water. 'That's better,' he said. 'Right. Two minutes and then we'll finish filming.'

'Will, I don't know what to say. I can't apologize enough,' Amber wailed.

'Let's not talk about it any more,' said Will. 'Time to wrap up the show.'

He walked over to where the camera had set up. 'Well, that's been one of the most eventful shows so far. Burned offerings, smoke alarms, and chillies pretending to be innocent tomatoes. Don't ever let anyone tell you kitchens are cosy places.' He gave the camera one of his gorgeous smiles.

'But now,' he went on, 'it's time to announce the results . . .'

Everyone shuffled about and crossed their fingers.

'In third place, with an imaginative variation on an old favourite, it's Michael Malone's Sausage and Baked-bean Pie.'

Michael smiled and punched the air with his fist, and we all clapped.

'And in second place, a recipe that takes an old classic and gives it a fun new twist. Rosie Stevens' Fizzy Apricot Pudding.'

Rosie gasped and I squealed, and everyone laughed and clapped again.

'And finally, the first prize. This was a very tough decision, with so many –' He caught sight of the vegetable and sausage jelly and looked a bit green for a moment – 'unusual dishes to choose from. But our winner shows that if you have a bit of imagination and a lot of style, you can come up with something great to eat against all odds. Yes, our winner is – Alexandra Bond. Up you come, Alex!'

I couldn't believe it. Everybody was clapping – even Pearl managed a couple of hand movements as the camera panned round. Rosie whooped and whistled.

Will handed me my prize – a big box of

What's Cooking, Will? goodies, wrapped up with a big red ribbon. Amber Barconi shook my hand. She was smiling for the cameras, but her face looked very strange. I think she was gritting her teeth.

Will waved and smiled, and then he turned to the camera to finish the show. 'Look out for all the winning recipes in the cookbook that accompanies the series – details coming up. And join us again next week for *What's Cooking, Will?* when we'll be looking at the essential birthday tea. Bye for now . . .'

'Bye!' we all shouted and waved at the camera. The director had told us to make it look 'spontaneous', but a lot of kids thought that just meant 'very loud'.

'Wow!' said Rosie. 'Our recipes are going to be in a Will Masters' cookbook! We're on our way to being famous chefs already!'

'Not me,' I said. 'Cooking is *way* too much like hard work. There are *loads* of other ways to be famous. I just need to find the right one!'

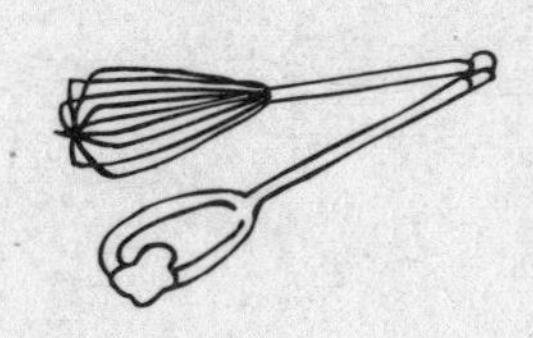

Postscript
Hiya! magazine

The star-studded cast of *Space-Shuttle Venus* tucked into an unearthly snack at the London premiere. (*Photos of glam people smiling into the camera – all with terribly stained teeth.)*

'I thought it tasted rather odd,' commented movie star Brace Manhattan. 'But I'd just come off my bananas diet, and I'd have eaten anything that looked a bit crunchy. I'll be talking to my lawyers.'

'I'm baffled by this most unfortunate incident, commented caterer-to-the-stars Amber Barconi. 'We will, of course, be investigating thoroughly.'

The offending dish, which turned guests' teeth black and green, arrived as part of the catering provided by Amber Nectar, the former top model's own company.

Alex's *Gateaux Aromatiques*

(Otherwise known as Smelly Cheese Scones)

Get together:
225 g self-raising flour (careful when you sieve it or you'll look like a ghost)
pinch of salt (never did get the hang of this)
50 g butter or margarine
25 g cheese, grated (watch you don't grate your fingers)
50 g dried dates, chopped really small
1 teaspoon ground cardamom
150 ml of milk

1. Heat up the oven to Gas 7 (about 220°C, Karim says).
2. Lightly grease a baking tray, ready to put the scones on.
3. Mix together the flour and salt and rub in the butter between your fingers. (The secret to getting scones rather than lumps is to keep going until the butter's all rubbed in and it all looks like breadcrumbs.)
4. Stir in the grated cheese and dates and cardamom, and splosh in the milk. Mix it all up until it's a soft dough.
5. Sprinkle some flour on to the work surface and put the dough on to it. Squeeze it for a bit and then pat it flat until it's about 2 cm thick.
6. Use a cutter to stamp out rounds and place them on the baking tray. Push the rest of the dough back together and stamp out more scones to use it all up.
7. Brush the tops of the scones with a little milk.
8. Bake for 12–15 minutes until well risen and golden.
9. Cool on a wire rack – then eat!

Alex's Alaska Surprise

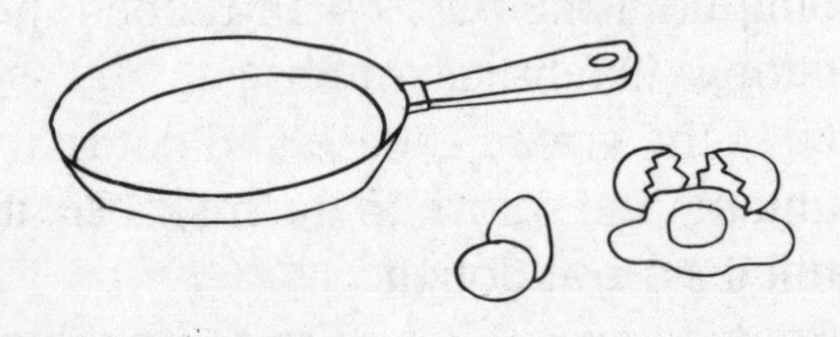

(Makes 2–3 sandwiches)

Get together:
2–3 eggs
2–3 tablespoons of milk
pinch of cinnamon and nutmeg (if you've got some!)
2 tablespoons any flavour jam
4–6 slices of white sliced bread (a day old is best)
vanilla ice cream (but any ice cream will do)
icing sugar
butter for frying

1. Beat the eggs and add the milk, cinnamon and nutmeg.
2. Heat the butter in a large frying pan. While it's heating, dip two slices of bread into the egg mix, making sure the bread is soaked all over.
3. Fry the bread on both sides – about 2–3 minutes each side.
4. Put one of the slices on a plate and spread it with jam.
5. Put a dollop of ice cream on the bread. Press the other slice down on top.
6. Dust with icing sugar. Repeat for more sandwiches.
7. Eat quickly – the ice cream melts!

WARNING: Don't attempt to make these recipes without adult supervision.